2024 STONE'S THROW

STONE'S THROW EDITOR: R.D. Sullivan
STONE'S THROW ANNUAL EDITOR: Paul J. Garth
RHP EDITOR-IN-CHIEF: Roger Nokes
MANAGING EDITOR: Jay Butkowski
CONTRIBUTING EDITOR: Albert Tucher
EDITOR: Rob D. Smith
ACQUISITION EDITOR: Ashley-Ruth M. Bernier
ACQUISITION EDITOR: Victor De Anda
ACQUISITION EDITOR: Susan Jessen
GUARDIAN ANGEL: Jonathan Elliott
COVER DESIGNER: Heather Garth

ON THE WEB: **www.rockandahardplacemag.com**
BY EMAIL: **editors@rockandahardplacemag.com**

Rock and a Hard Place Magazine is a labor of love, produced by a team of volunteer editors to showcase the best in dark fiction, crime, dystopian fiction, and noir. To learn how you can support the mission of **Rock and a Hard Place Press** through tax-deductible donations, or by subscribing to the RHP Patreon, please visit the website, and click "**Support RHP**" through the main menu.

Print ISBN: 979-8-9912950-3-1

eBook ISBN: 979-8-9912950-4-8

Published by Rock and a Hard Place Press, an imprint of Rock and a Hard Place Press, LLC, Woodbridge, NJ.
rockandahardplacemag.com
amazon.com/Rock-and-a-Hard-Place-Press

Follow us on Social Media:
https://www.facebook.com/RHP.books/
https://www.instagram.com/rhp.press/
https://www.threads.net/@rhp.press
https://bsky.app/profile/rhppress.bsky.social
https://x.com/RHP_Press

Contents

Foreword

Here we are again. Once more 'round the sun. Another journey completed. Another begun. And, as always, we enter the new year with stories behind us and the knowledge that there are more yet to be told.

I'm thinking of cycles, as I write this. As I type, it's late at night on one of the earliest days of January, a brand new year waiting to bloom in front of us, and, though you and I may hope whatever is coming in 2025 will be surprising and warm and beautiful, full of compassion and inspiration, the dark and cold outside my window suggests it's fine to hope, but foolish to believe. The sun rises, but it sets as well. People try their best but fail. The cycles go on and on, waiting for someone with the strength to break them. When those breakthroughs come, we celebrate them as proof that the cyclical nature of everything isn't what we think it is, that it can be broken, that our lives are ours alone and can be lived however we see fit. But the sun always sets. The year always turns over. The cycles continue, gripping us in their currents and pulling us along.

If that weren't true, you wouldn't be holding this copy of ***Stone's Throw Annual 2024*** in your hands right now.

I've long thought that, if writing is the act of confronting the truth of the world, the act of reading is to wallow in it; to sift through the murk, searching for those stories or phrases of even just, sometimes, a singular, perfectly chosen word that connects us to the writer, that tells us, yes, this person sees the truth just as I do.

Ultimately, that's what **Stone's Throw** is. Every month, we provide writers with a prompt. These prompts are usually seasonal, but they're also always based on something we've been thinking about, a fear we're facing, or a truth we're considering, or an implication that's been left hanging by some other story, and then we read the submissions, looking for the truth.

And the truths you'll find in the pages that follow. Cycles of abuse, moving from one person to the next. The seasonal changes that bring secrets to the surface. The huge power of tiny individuals with the barest authority. The determination to persist, even after the most shattering of tragedies. The blossoming and disillusionment of love. The indestructibility of rats. And so much more.

Every single one of the stories that follows has something special in it. A truth that made us message each other and say, "this is it. This is exactly what we're looking for." Every single one of these stories has touched us, in some way, and we believe you'll find something in them, too. The truth, most likely.

And when you're done, once you've read through a full year's worth of stories, we'll be at the end of another cycle, hopefully one that doesn't break. And again, next year, we'll be back. The cycle will continue again. Stories behind us, and new ones yet to be told.

Once more 'round the sun.

-Paul J. Garth
Stone's Throw Editor
January 2, 2025

JANUARY 2024 PROMPT – Nothing like success to breed hubris, eh? As we welcome 2024 to our doorsteps, send us your best story of it happening again, of characters emboldened by previous success, and how this new-found confidence might be the very thing that brings something—them, their job, others—to their knees.

Canary in the Coal Mine

Sally Milliken

"I'm the queen of the world," I shouted to the sky with my arms outstretched. From the highest ledge above the old rock quarry, I reigned over everyone and everything. My long, wet hair fanned across my shoulders while my favorite bikini—bright canary yellow—reflected in the sun. I shook my head, the water droplets landing on the granite under my feet like a Jackson Pollock painting. I waved to my boyfriend, Hunter, who had been watching from the far side of the quarry with the cooler of beer and a small flock of high school friends.

I'd done it. I'd jumped from Tower Rock. No one in our generation had ever done it before. I'd gone off to college while the others stayed home—to work at fast food restaurants and mall chain stores—and I'd returned for the summer broke and exhausted, needing to prove that I could do anything.

I'd never forget that feeling of weightlessness as I fell through the air after my feet left the granite point, as if time stood still. I'd never felt so in control and invincible, like how birds must feel as they ruled the sky. I'd landed in the water with my arms tight across my chest to hold on my suit. My feet had cut through the surface with only a slight splash just as I'd planned. I'd forced myself not to gasp with shock from the frigid water hitting my face. After I'd popped up to the surface, I'd whooped. The audience had cheered.

I'd quickly swum to a shallow ledge and scrambled out of the water to bask in the praise from my friends. Slipping slightly in my haste when I'd stepped in a vein of mud between the rocks, I'd stubbed my toe on a sharp edge. I hadn't even felt the pain.

The first jump was for them, the next would be for me. My friend Ava waved from below and toasted me with her bottle of suntan oil. The scent of coconut was strong and the smell hung in the air. I returned her grin and responded from my high perch with a matching toast with my bottle of vodka.

I wrapped my mouth around the lip of the bottle and took a long swig. Damn. It was empty. I tossed it over the edge, to join the other hundreds of bottles and cans deep down in the water-filled pit. Ava, Hunter, and I tried to reach the bottom one year, holding our breath dive after dive, but we never did.

"Aren't you going next, Ava?" I yelled to her, waving my hand to encourage her. "If I can do it, you can."

"Nah, I'm better with my feet on the ground. I'm not crazy like you." Ava hugged herself, one hand dropping to cup her belly, a movement visible even from my height. I'd noticed a similar gesture a few days before and wondered if she was knocked up. She'd been vague for the past few months when I'd asked her if she'd been seeing anyone. *I'll ask her about it again later*, I promised myself. We used to tell each other everything but since I'd been gone, keeping secrets from each other seemed to be another change in our friendship.

"Holy shit, you did it," Hunter said, his eyes wide as his shaggy head appeared from the rocks below. After dropping our bags, he hugged me from behind, his arms encircling my body with a towel. "That was awesome. I can't believe you did it."

Turning in his arms, I grabbed him by the neck and pulled his face down for a sloppy kiss. I'd missed the warmth of his lips on mine.

"You look hot," he groaned. He rubbed my arms and played with the strings holding on my suit. "No freshmen fifteen for you." Taking a step back, he pulled a can of Bud from his pocket, took a sip, and then handed it to me. "I've missed you."

"Me too. Long distance sucks." I hugged him again, speaking into his soft flannel shirt. "Do you know what's up with Ava? She's not acting herself. I guess, quieter than usual."

"She seems fine to me. I'm sure it's nothing. Probably just adjusting to having you back in town."

"That must be it." I took another sip, grimacing as the bitter flavor slipped down my throat.

"Come on up," Hunter yelled to the others. "Bring the cooler with you."

Five minutes later, Ava pulled herself to the granite shelf. Two other friends appeared just after, struggling with the cooler. I could hear the cans sliding around along with the ice inside accompanied by cursing and laughter. Hunter snagged one of the handles and helped lower the cooler to the rock ledge.

I spread an old quilt next to the cooler. I pushed a beer into Ava's hands and laughed as Hunter pulled me down into his lap. Ava sat on the other side of Hunter watching us.

"I'm going to try a backflip next time," I whispered after I nibbled his earlobe.

"I'd like to see that." Hunter gave me a long open-mouthed kiss. "You're my hero."

I waggled my eyebrows toward Ava as I curled my hands around Hunter's warm cheeks to kiss him again. Shaking her head, she rolled her eyes and slid further away from us. I sighed and snuggled closer into his body for warmth.

My older sister was the one who had first told me how to scramble up the bank of Tower Rock for the right launch location. She'd described how to use the roots of a large tree as a handle to get out far enough over the water so that the jumper wouldn't hit the rocks jutting out on the way down or the hidden rocks under the surface. It was just as she described. I'd had to sidestep along the ledge, using the root of a stunted pine as a handle, smoothed by all the hands that had gone before. Others had gotten that far and turned back. But not me.

"You going again?" Ava asked and began to chant. "Jump! Jump! Jump!" The others all joined in, clapping, and hollering.

Tossing off the towel, I kissed Hunter hard on the lips, took a large swig of his beer, gave a flourishing bow to the entire group, and made my way back to the launch spot.

Flattening myself along the cliff edge, I sidestepped slowly to the jump-off point. My heart pounded with adrenaline. This would be the best backflip ever. Epic, even. They'd be talking about it for years after. I'd become legendary, like the generation before us, the ones who'd first jumped from this spot. Turning to face the cliff, I carefully placed my toes in a secure niche, with my heels extended over nothing but air.

Ava counted down. "Three, two, one."

I bent my knees slightly and leaned back. I was ready. Just a little more leverage on the branch and then...

My hand slipped. Where I'd been holding that hand-slicked root moments before, I now only grasped air. Weight already shifted back, I tried to grab again as I started falling.

Clawing frantically for a hold, fingertips brushed the cliff and the wood, and then nothing.

I heard a gasp. Was it me? Or someone else? As I fell, the audience went quiet. The forest went silent. No sound of birds. No branches rustling in the wind.

Time stood still once more. All I could do was desperately twist in the air and try to fling myself farther from the cliff wall. I felt the blood spurt from my head on the first hit. I tumbled down. And down. The last thing I remembered was the smell of coconut oil tickling my nose as I tried to protect my skull from bashing the unforgiving rocks below.

SALLY MILLIKEN (Instagram: @sallyhistorymystery) writes contemporary and historical mysteries and crime fiction. Besides finding creative ways to bring villains to justice, she enjoys bending clay to her will on the pottery wheel and shooting pucks on net with her ice hockey team. Her stories have been published online and in various anthologies. The flash fiction story "Adam-13" was the 2023 winner of the Golden Donut Award. She also won first prize in the 2023 Bethlehem Writers Story Contest. She is working on her first novel, a historical mystery set in 1882 Massachusetts. Find her at https://www.sallymillikenauthor.com/. Sally is a member of Sisters in Crime, Sisters in Crime NE, SinC Guppy Chapter, MWA, and the Short Mystery Fiction Society.

FEBRUARY 2024 PROMPT — The coldest months are here, and with them, we're thinking of all those frozen things, just waiting to thaw out. This month, send us your best story about something that's been on ice for too long—a secret, a relationship, a memory, a lie, or anything else that can be frozen away. And then tell us what happens when it finally starts to thaw.

Deer Tracks

M.E. Proctor

There was a story Willie remembered hearing at the Pit Stop, of a man found frozen on a mountain. At first, folks thought he might have been an alpinist or a hiker gone missing in a storm, but it turned out he was from a thousand years ago, and he'd been beaten up and killed. Or he died from hunger and exposure. The Pit Stop regulars had debated the topic for hours, as they tended to do, because they loved arguing, and there was little else available in town in the way of entertainment. Willie didn't recall how the story went, and he wasn't going to look it up on his phone. Everything you did on these machines was recorded somewhere, that's what Morris from the Pit Stop said, and Morris was a fool but that didn't mean he was always wrong. It didn't hurt to be careful.

The snow overnight reminded Willie of the old iceman, even if the two-inch-thick layer that coated his land didn't compare to what fell in the mountains. He expected the stuff to stick for a few days. The ground was frozen solid, had been for almost three weeks, which was unheard of in these parts. It messed up the roads and kept people snug at home. Pretty quiet all around. Not that Willie expected anybody to visit. And he certainly didn't want anybody to visit unexpected. He'd made it clear that he wanted to be left alone. Most of the time, people complied.

The crisp cold air, the blue sky, and the white powder made the old farm and the fields pretty as a postcard. All the rusty crap going back years that Willie had never bothered to pick up was blanketed and the view was much improved. The snow was undisturbed, except for a line of tracks as precise as stitches on a freshly laundered linen tablecloth. The deer had come close to the farm, looking for something to munch on.

Willie had spotted two does at the edge of the woods this morning and it made him curious to see where they'd been exploring. He bundled up, took his sturdy cane, and followed the tracks. They were all over the wide-open north field, delicate and jumpy, like the deer had been having fun dancing in the frosty fluff. He followed the elegant hoof tracks all the way to the frozen pond where the animals must have lingered. The snowy crust was trampled.

Something in the pond, under the thick lid of ice, caught his eye.

He stuck his cane in the spiky clumps of grass for balance and leaned forward to get a better look. The sight made him take a step back and he almost lost his footing. His breath caught, a sudden clamp on his throat. He fought for a wheezing gulp of air and grasped his cane tighter.

Goddamit. He didn't need the aggravation.

He glanced around, squinting in the bright light. He was alone. A handful of crows strutted on the other side of the pond, involved in a shrill argument he wasn't part of.

Maybe the deer had spotted the same thing he saw under the perfect blue mirror of the pond, glossy and unbroken except for the old duck house half collapsed in the middle. He wondered what the animals thought about it. Were they scared? Had they reared back in alarm, like he did?

It was strange how the snow didn't stick on the frozen pond. Maybe the water still retained some of the warmth of the fall. That was a disturbing thought, the possibility of captive heat under the ice. With what was down there . . . Willie's knuckles whitened on the cane.

"Get a grip," he grumbled.

The sight gave him a shock, but it wasn't anything to be afraid of. Bernie Cullen wasn't going to rise from the depth, break the ice, and grab him by the ankles. He was as dead and frozen as that primitive mountain man from long ago.

Willie forced himself to look in Bernie's pale eyes, took in the guy's familiar stupid fat face as round as the moon. It seemed intact. Bernie looked smarter in death than he'd ever been alive. Like he was reflecting before uttering words of wisdom. Willie chuckled. Right, as if Bernie ever thought twice before spitting insanities. The problem with Bernie was that he could never keep his damn mouth shut. Words drooled out of him like snuff juice. Dangerous words that had consequences. It was like what they said during the war that Willie's dad went overseas to fight: Loose lips sink ships.

Bernie's loose mouth could have sent Willie to that old red brick house in Huntsville.

A bullet silenced him. A cinder block should have kept him at the bottom of the pond. What the hell was he doing up, with his frozen fat face sticking to the underside of the ice?

"Wanna tell me a tale, Bern?" Willie croaked. His throat prickled with the last shreds of the head cold he caught while waiting for Bernie to come back to his camp after a day of hunting. Rainy, windy, and dark. Wreaked hell on his arthritis. Twisted his back too, when he'd heaved the body into the truck. The pain laid him low for a week. Bernie was the misery that kept on giving. Damn nuisance. The chain that tied him to the cinder block must have slipped. Willie was dog-tired when he worked on that. Must have made a mistake.

He secured the cane more firmly and bent over, one hand on a bony knee for extra support. He'd never noticed that Bernie had so much hair on his head. Probably because he always wore that greasy John Deere ballcap. Was it true that hair kept growing after death? The gray tendrils on the side of Bernie's head moved with the current of the spring that fed the pond. It was uncanny how well preserved the wretched bugger was. The fish and turtles, or even the occasional resident gator waddling over to the pond from the nearby lake should have made quick work of the asshole. The unexpected cold snap threw things off.

Nature. Never going the way you wanted. Too hot, too cold, too wet, too dry. The eternal punishment of the farmer. A good thing that Willie wasn't growing anything anymore. He was done worrying about the weather. A guy from the other side of town came for the hay and split the profits with him. It helped with the bills. Not that Willie needed much to get by. There was enough left of Marion's money to last to the end.

The goddam money that he thought was a blessing, coming in like that, just when his body decided it had taken its fill of abuse. The money Marion inherited from a forgotten aunt, out of the blue. Now they could enjoy the land, he told Marion. Watch the deer and the change of season. We deserve to rest, my beloved.

She didn't want to hear any of it.

It was their chance to get away from the lousy farm, she said. "Sell the land, Willie," she nagged. His land. Where his parents were buried, his grans, his brother, the baby they lost when they were newly married. The blood, the sweat, the ache. His land. Leave it for what? A town of brick and concrete, sickly trees and flea-infested pigeons?

They fought. They screamed at each other, worse than they ever did. She said she would go, with the money and without him. He lost his temper. Damn, he always had a temper, and he was stubborn, had to be, to work this land that was hard clay and as hardheaded as he was.

Willie's gaze drifted from ghostly Bernie making faces at him from under the ice to the crumbling duck house. Marion was down there. What was left of her, which couldn't be much after all the years. It reminded him of his panic during the big drought, when the lake dropped four feet, and talk of what was uncovered was all over the county. Sunken boats, farm equipment from before the lake was filled, pieces of the old railroad tracks, vehicle carcasses—didn't they find a body in one of them? Willie checked on the pond every day during that blasted summer. He watched the pool level diminish, saw the spring shrink to a sweaty shine on the mud, measured the cracks on the bottom, filled his nostrils with the stench of rotting fish, and waited to see bones, white as bleached wood poking through the muck. Marion encased in red clay.

He feared he'd have to walk out there, sink up to his knees in that rotten deposit of time, and break Marion's bones to shards with a shovel.

But the pond was deep there in the middle, and Marion's resting place was secure. Then the rain came and the pond filled up again. That was twelve years ago, and the pond never got that low again.

How Bernie got it in his head that Marion hadn't left, like Willie told whoever asked, would forever be a mystery. Bernie had a bit of a storyteller reputation at the Pit Stop. His yarns didn't amount to much, an amusement for the evening between cards and football on TV. Good for a laugh or a shiver. He must have had a crush on Marion because he kept bringing her up in conversation every chance he got. Willie told him to stop, that her leaving him still hurt, no matter how many years had gone by, and for a little while Bernie took heed. Till he got back on the subject again and Willie knew he had to put an end to it.

Willie tapped the ice with the cane. It made a dull sound, like a full barrel.

The crows were still haggling, irritating in their insistence to be noticed.

Willie knew how the next days would roll. It was a repeat of the drought. Worry would drive him to check on Bernie, knowing full well that nothing would change—the eyes, the face, the hair. Not until the thaw, and then the stench, until the body rotted and sank.

He didn't have the patience for it.

He trudged back to the farm to get tools.

***

A blizzard blew down from Canada that night and the temperature dropped another ten degrees. It was much worse in the open fields where the wind whipped at will, unhindered by trees. Records were broken. Thermometers burst, according to Morris. The regulars at the Pit Stop agreed. It was a devilish night, all right, the night Willie died. Heart attack, the doc said.

The Pit Stop guys couldn't figure what'd got into the old man.

Some said it was because of the deer. That he went to break the ice to give them running water. And there sure were lots of tracks around the pond. Others commented that Willie was a little off. Hadn't been right in the head since Marion left all these years ago. Being solitary like he was. That couldn't be good for a man. Made him odd.

If the mail lady hadn't decided to brave the black ice, fallen trees, and snow-choked country roads to deliver a package that had sat at the post office for a week, Willie might have been left out there a long time. The Pit Stop commentators concurred that it would have been a horrible thing. Animals got hungry this time of year. The old men contemplated that predicament with frowns and head shakes.

Then the conversation shifted to Bernie Cullen, whom none of them had seen in a while. He must still be at his deer lease, dedicated hunter that he was.

"Willie dying like that all of a sudden. That'll give him a shock," Morris said.

Sure would.

M.E. PROCTOR (Substack: https://meproctor.substack.com/; Website: https://shawmystery.com/) was born in Brussels and lives in Texas. The first book in her Declan Shaw PI series, *Love You Till Tuesday*, came out from Shotgun Honey with a follow up scheduled for 2025. She's the author of a short story collection, *Family and Other Ailments*. Her fiction has appeared in various crime anthologies and magazines like *Vautrin, Bristol Noir, Mystery Tribune, Shotgun Honey, Reckon Review,* and *Black Cat Weekly.*

ROCK AND A HARD PLACE
MAGAZINE

Issues 1-12 available now!
www.rockandahardplacemag.com

MARCH 2023 PROMPT — A time for renewal and celebration. A time for all that death to be swept away. But not here. This month, we're looking for stories of people who refuse to deal with the reality of their situation, and how their denial leads them to triumph, or doom, or, maybe, acceptance.

Alan and Felix

L.P. Ring

When Alan lost his first tooth, Felix wedged out his own with pliers from the toolbox beneath the sink. He bled all down his white t-shirt, leaving splotches on the linoleum and cabinets that near gave Mom a heart attack when she brought in the washing. When Felix got picked for football, Alan practised every evening after homework until he got picked too. When Felix had his first kiss, lost his virginity, had his first break-up, Alan wasn't far behind. When Alan took evening tuition to secure his A-levels, Felix did too. They aced their exams but went to a local Polytechnic to stay close to Mom. She was ill two years by then.

Big brother Felix didn't labour being fourteen minutes older too often, having promised Mom he wouldn't pick on his brother before cancer took her just shy of their nineteenth birthday. But he did like keeping score, keeping things competitive.

Competition brought out the best in them.

Felix's first was sloping between the library stacks, ferreting for an Isak Dinesen collection for her Early 20th Century Lit. class. She had lank black hair like a Bassett Hound's ears, glass lenses thick enough to stand a coke on, and mommy and daddy's chip-shop bulk. She stood transfixed while Felix discussed *Out of Africa*—he'd seen the movie—endearingly incognizant of the line this God was spinning her. Few men paid attention to Shirley Harris, let alone a third-year from the university rugby team whose upper arms stretched his t-shirt's fabric close to tearing. She stuttered an acceptance when he invited her for cheeseburgers—his guilty pleasure—after the library shut.

She'd have died of embarrassment at the secondary school portrait her parents chose for her missing person's poster.

Alan sat across from his choice at lunch three days later. "You're not picking a date," he remembered Felix warning him. "Get someone nobody'll remember."

His choice was unsuitable enough—tall, willowy, with a brush of nose freckles and breathlessly blonde hair flowing between her shoulders. But when Alan carried her books to her next class, Felix could've chased him down the corridor and throttled him. "I'll pick someone else," Alan yelled later, smouldering in the passenger seat of Mom's battered Ford Sierra.

"No blondes," Felix sniped as they weaved past rear traffic lights set red and sullen in the twilight. Bruno Brooks was talking up the upcoming 600th Number One and Felix let out an "Oh bloody shut up!" and switched off the radio. "Dark. Plain. Frumpy. Blondes attract attention. Blondes bring Candlelit Vigils and headline news." The slur he used next made Alan blanch.

"Mom would slap your mouth for saying that."

"Mom's dead two years and like the movie, 'I ain't afraid of no ghosts.' Fuck whatever Mom would say."

Later, Alan knew that was when they started drifting. Yet soon after, with the ground almost too frozen to dig and the wind ripping the few leaves left from the trees, a first-year disappeared cutting through a park after dark. And, perhaps initially as a middle finger to Felix, Alan kept seeing the blonde. Six months later, Shirley Harris was a tattered page on a lamp post only her parents mourned and gossipy neighbours remembered. Alan's eventual choice never warranted proper attention. The police, seeing education but also colour, never considered the two disappearances together.

Both brothers graduated with honours. Felix got a position in the City and pestered his younger brother to follow. Alan talked up local growth, quibbled over the salary a similar City concern offered, and thought about the blonde a year from finishing her teaching degree. One night they exchanged gasps of "I love you" between fumbled, sweat-slicked trysts.

Felix smashed a glass off the kitchen wall. "I said choose a kill, not a fucking wife. You think she'd stay with you long if she knew how close she was to being on the evening news?!"

Alan reckoned she never would know unless Felix wanted company in Wakefield Prison.

Felix left, Alan stayed, did the books for a local builder, and eyed a three-bed on the outskirts of town. Felix wrote letters with fleeting mentions to women's names as rarely repeated as orchids bloom—letters which were turned to ash via the embers of a cigarette in the back yard after Alan finished downing a couple of cans.

Alan went down on one knee during a weekend away in Paris. When he told his brother, Felix said what happened to Mom and Dad would happen to Alan as well—they were their mother's sons, weren't they?—and hung up without another word.

Alan gripped the phone, remembering the time they'd come home from training early to find Mom struggling with a guy she'd picked up hitchhiking. The kitchen knife was embedded deep enough in his neck for the blade's point to stick out the other side. She sent them both to their room, though Felix kept sneaking down to see what she was doing. Eventually, Alan found out from whispered exchanges beneath the covers, she'd needed Felix's help.

On their wedding day, Felix sent a bouquet signed by him and someone named Monica, citing a previously booked trip abroad. "This must be serious," Alan's now wife remarked, seeing how Felix's brush-off stung. "He's taking her for a week away."

Alan's library visit waited until after the honeymoon. The names from Felix's letters, burned into his treacherous memory, were all there in the blurred microfiche of missing persons dotted up and down the country. Probably soon to be joined by Monica from the bouquet who might not have even made it back from their trip. Alan finished his searches, dropped into a nearby off-licence for a bottle of whiskey, and drove to a forest a few short miles from their old campus. He'd been right about a phone box being there and the phone at the other end of the line rang and rang. Finally, his brother picked up. He might have just been running.

"Felix?"

"Persistent bugger, aren't you? What do you want, little brother?"

"I'm over at the old campus, next to that woodland. Do you remember her?"

"I remember mine. All she wanted out of life was to be an English teacher and eat fast food. God, what a waste of a life that would have been."

"How's Monica?"

"How's your wife?"

"This needs to stop, Felix." The thought of Felix getting caught and destroying both of them threatened to leap from his lips but he managed to choke it down. He didn't want to sound like a coward. He refused to be the type of person who only cared about his own lousy skin. Refused to appear that way to Felix.

"Careful, Alan. Remember old memories can poison your present. As can threatening me." There was a click and Alan was alone with a dial tone.

He sat in his car until the bottle was half-drank, listening to Capital Radio and staring into the trees. Ignoring the dog walkers, ramblers, and teenagers that gawped at the weird guy just sitting behind the wheel getting wasted. Flecks of snow danced from the deep grey sky, disappearing into the ground, or dying on the windscreen.

He thought of his only attempt at a kill, how she wriggled from his half-hearted grasp and ran.

How Felix chased her down, dragged her into the forest. Made him stab her the final time.

He pictured the ground beneath the 100-plus-year-old oak where he'd buried her alone.

That night, he remembered, each time he'd forced the shovel's blade into the earth, he'd been certain that a cop, security guard, or even just an unlucky forest rambler would come across him finishing his grisly task. He remembered the relief he felt patting down that final shovelful of clay. Walking away, he'd promised himself he'd never return here.

As he finally relented and screwed the cap back on the bottle, he realized that being found then would have been the best thing of all. It would have stopped Felix. It would have saved the blonde from marrying him too.

He and Felix no longer did everything in unison. But big brother wouldn't quit keeping score. Alan retrieved the shovel he'd stuck in the trunk that morning and, burnished both against the cold and the prospect of punishment by the whiskey, stalked into the forest. Back to where his youth ended, where this road to destruction began.

He kept insisting to himself that the grave wouldn't be hard to find, that his memory would stand him in good stead. And then he would drive to the station, admit everything. Tell the police where to find the body. Tell them Felix's address. He couldn't change the past. And the present was well and truly poisoned. But he could save at least some of the future.

L.P. RING (Twitter / X: @L_P_Ring; BlueSky: @lpring.bsky.social) has been living outside his native Ireland for the past twenty years. He's had fiction published with *Black Beacon*, *Shotgun Honey*, *Chthonic Matters*, and *Creepy Podcast* among others. He lives in Japan with his wife and a cat which is always around at mealtimes.

Floating Blossoms on Still Water

Russell Thayer

Pauline drifted on her back in the sun. Bruised legs spread wide. Still as death. The water in the bay rolled with delicate swells, which sometimes broke over her chin. She dared not choke or sputter as she drew slow breaths. They might hear. The soldiers on the beach who had marched the able-bodied men around the headland to be shot, returning with blood and lust on their haughty faces. Afterwards, the women were made to wade into the surf, stopping when the water reached their waists. An officer then ordered them to face the sea as the team set up its machine gun.

She floated, a bullet gone straight through her, tendrils of Beryl's long red hair tangled in her curled fingers.

Evelyn's head nestled into Pauline's armpit. They'd met at school in Ballarat. Her oldest friend in the Australian Army Nursing Service. Their fingers sometimes brushed as the waves rocked them together. Others had died holding hands. Sister Rubina and Sister Lorna. Ada and Olive hung in the water near Pauline, hand in hand.

For a bright young woman from New South Wales, born on a sheep station populated with rough, uneducated men, the AANS had been a romantic dream. A way out of the dry life. A path to adventure. After extensive training, Pauline was sent to Singapore for nursing experience, then to a field hospital near Bakri when war broke out. When defeat was the only clear outcome, she was sent back to Singapore to await her fate.

Perhaps Minnie or Ellen would float by. Her best girlfriends. The two who always joined Pauline for a beer and a smoke on warm nights in hot clubs, eyes keen for men who could dance. She recalled their visits to Chinese photographic exhibitions and Happy World amusement park. The three of them should have been holding hands as the bullets came, just as they did sometimes while marching half-drunk around the waterfront. If those girls would glide by, she'd pull them close, making a raft of memories, of feng, laksa, and bak kut teh purchased from market stalls. Kaya toast with afternoon tea. What would her mother think of that? After raising her daughter on mutton and potatoes. What would her mother think of her now?

Pauline hadn't seen Mona since the evacuation ship was split in two by Japanese airplanes. The screams of children still echoed in her submerged ears. Many of the nurses had died before the survivors took to the boats. Mona didn't make it. Mona, who had taken photography classes with Pauline at a Japanese studio near Queen Street. They'd purchased cameras together, and would explore the Singapore neighborhoods looking for exotic flowers to capture on film. In still life. Pauline had won a competition with a mounted photo called "Lipstick Plant in Water on Bedside Table." Her commanding officer got word of the prize and complained that the photo displayed a phallic eroticism unbecoming a woman serving in the AANS. The officer hadn't gotten word of the brazen night Pauline and Mona photographed each other in the nude, in a hotel room, later developing the pictures in secret during time rented at the studio where they studied their artistic diversion.

Then there was Cedric. An English doctor with a trim beard and black hair, a man who liked tall, awkward girls with pale coloring and sandy locks. He wouldn't be floating by.

"We should wait," she'd told him, unsure about giving her virginity away to a near stranger in his rooms, hungry hands pulling at her clothing until she stormed out. Angry. Cold. Had she waited too long, she wondered, finding out on the dock that he wasn't coming, that he was butchered with all the other medical personnel at Alexandra Barracks Hospital?

What would he think of her now, torn apart as she was?

To stop dwelling on the pain and the bacteria that washed into her wound with every roll of the teeming sea, Pauline considered the island where she would die. Where was this place? It had felt like paradise the few hours she'd spent on the white sand drinking fresh water carried by men from a nearby brook while she attended to other men who couldn't walk. She knew the evacuation ship had gone down while they were still east of Sumatra, but she wished she'd been told the name of the island, remaining motionless as she listened to the screams of the men who couldn't walk being bayonetted one after the other. The men in her care. She wondered what had gone through their minds as the two dozen nurses were raped in front of them.

Eventually, the soldiers collected the machine gun and left the gutted men on the sand. Turning her head slightly to the side, Pauline watched until the setting sun moved over a clump of red-trunked trees in bloom. She lifted her head to scan the deserted landscape, feeling her legs sink. She could see where the bullet had come out through her diaphragm. She'd treated many wounds just like hers. Men who had lived.

Wondering when other creatures would come to taste her flesh, or when her blood would finish bubbling out of her, she noticed something in the trees. A man hobbled onto the deserted beach, ruining the still life she would have called "Dead Men on White Sand". He was one of the able-bodied men that had been taken out of view and shot. Gripping his stomach, he dropped to his knees next to the bodies of his comrades. Maybe the photo wouldn't be ruined.

The rosy color of the vast sky, clouds gathering in the east, made her lower her head back into the water. She was ready to float away under such beauty.

But the man had gotten to his feet again. Pauline could hear him crashing into shallow water. She lifted her head to watch him discover the half-dressed female bodies that had drifted to shore. He'd staggered back to this stretch of sand because he remembered the nurses, that they had set up shop here. On the beach. The tarp still rippled, flapping in the trees. The banner with the red cross crudely painted on it hung from the tarp. She could see the supplies in canvas rucksacks.

The man needed help. Perhaps he was a good man. Pauline smacked her palm onto the surface of the water to attract his attention, her feet touching the sandy bottom. He splashed in, but fell, crawling back to dry ground, clutching his abdomen.

Moving her arms, still life in her, she rose and waded toward shore. And duty.

RUSSELL THAYER's (Twitter / X: @RussellThayer10) work has appeared in *Brushfire, Tough*, Roi Fainéant Press, *Guilty Crime Magazine, Mystery Tribune, Close to the Bone, Bristol Noir, Apocalypse Confidential*, Cowboy Jamboree Press, *Hawaii Pacific Review, Shotgun Honey, A Thin Slice of Anxiety*, **Rock and a Hard Place Press**, *Revolution John, Punk Noir*, Expat Press, *Pulp Modern, The Yard Crime Blog*, and Outcast Press. He received his B.A. in English from the University of Washington, worked for decades at large printing companies, and currently lives in Missoula, Montana.

ROCK AND A HARD PLACE

LIKE WHAT YOU'RE READING?

YOU CAN HELP US CONTINUE TO PUBLISH THE BEST NOIR AND CRIME FICTION
AROUND BY JOINING OUR PATREON TEAM!

YOU'LL GAIN ACCESS TO BEHIND-THE-SCENE EXTRAS,
INTERVIEWS WITH OUR WRITERS,
SHOUT OUTS IN OUR BOOKS
AND MORE!

SIGN UP TODAY AT PATREON.COM/JOIN/RHPMAG

Alfred

John Bovio

Alfred had a New York abrasiveness many took for arrogance. They weren't wrong. The rumor was that he was freakishly endowed. The outline on his jeans suggested this very well could be true.

Before coming to Amsterdam, I moved from place to place, trying to outrun the feeling that I wasn't welcome anywhere before realizing I wasn't. Here, I found a city that embraced people who had worn out their welcome in other parts of the world. Alfred, too, fits in this category. He had a personality that gnawed on people like a rat.

***

Rats' front teeth grow 5 inches a year. They wear them down by continuously gnawing at everything around them.

Alfred had a bar in the Red Light District called the Oranje Krush. I heard he was a bit of a shitbag and had just fired his cook. I knew how to cook and needed a job, having just been let go from the Budget Hotel for my hair.

Yes. I had worn out my welcome again.

The short story is this: Queen's Day, Koninginnedag, in Amsterdam is a Carnival-like event at the end of April that attracts upwards of a quarter million people. The world's biggest party is a combination street fair, market, and music festival. Orange is the color of the Dutch Royal Family, who hails from the House of Oranje. The color has come to symbolize the country and signify national pride.

I decided to dye my hair orange for the event. Get my hair shaved up underneath, a little orange on top. The chemicals soon cooked my hair to a bone white, creating a fresh canvas for the vibrant color. The stylist mixed coral red and canary yellow Crazy Color and applied it to my head. When the cloud of chemicals cleared, my hair was the bright neon orange of a traffic safety cone. Given my commitment to the holiday, I was pretty popular on the day of the event, but some people can only appreciate this type of dedication at the moment.

The following day at work, the cleaning ladies gave me the stink eye. Then gossiped about me. Then bugged Nick until he had no choice but to fire me. I thought he was kidding, given how long I worked there. Joke was on me. I filled my backpack. Spit out, alone again. On my way out, Nick came through the side door and stopped me at the top of the stairs.

"I'm sorry," he said, "I couldn't . . ." Tears rolled down his cheeks, and he pushed a small roll of bills into my hand.

Loneliness was a companion that got me into more trouble than love.

***

A rat can fall 50 feet and not be injured.

I went to see Hans, who was renting a barge behind Centraal Station. He let me stay in the hold of the big steel beast. No heat, electricity, or water, but it was shelter. I used the money Nick gave me for self-medication medication. I went to see that cocksucker Jimmy who always shorted me. Sometimes you need a crooked guy to get straight.

***

Rats don't sweat. They constrict or expand the blood vessels in their tails to regulate their temperature.

That's what brought me to Alfred and the Oranje Krush. Circumstances being what they were, I needed to keep my head afloat.

***

A rat can tread water for three days as well as survive being flushed down the toilet.

"Make me something to eat," Alfred said when I asked for a job, his crotch bulging at me, a trouser snake of uncharmed vulgarity.

"Nice hair," Wolfgang, the hash dealer, said from his seat at the end of the bar as I made my way to the kitchen. Hash dealers, like gunfighters, always sit where they can see the whole room and never with their backs to the door.

I found potatoes, butter, milk, flour, and cheese in the kitchen. Of course, there was cheese; it's Holland, it grows on trees. The potatoes had taken up residency at the bar. They had fewer eyes than a scallop but more than a spider. I detected a slight smell of rot, but it was not from the potatoes. I made a roux with the flour and butter and soon had a cheese sauce for the two small casseroles of scalloped potatoes I made. Alfred said the potatoes were dry but gave me a job anyway.

***

Rats eat their own feces for nutritional value.

Wolfgang was a German hippy, hash-selling gangster. His shoulder-length brown hair found a part in the middle, and a gunfighter's mustache sat above his thin lips. He wore a white tunic with angel sleeves draped over skinny jeans fastened by a double O-ring studded leather belt. Jeans tucked into fringed suede boots. He carried a leather man purse with compartments like a file folder. Each compartment held a different kind of hash—Afghani Black, Indian Charis, Kashmiri, Red Lebanese, Nepalese Temple Ball, and Moroccan Honey. The only customers were for the hash. People didn't even stay to have a smoke. They came and went. They liked Wolfgang's hash but didn't like Alfred's attitude. No one tried my food. The potatoes grew more eyes.

***

Rats have belly buttons.

I spent the first three days cleaning the kitchen from top to bottom, chasing an odor that continued to get stronger despite my efforts. It was as if my elbow grease was rubbing a genie's lamp full of stink. On the fourth day, Alfred confessed. Told me about the rat problem. "It's why we have no customers." He had thrown a bunch of poison down in the basement. He wanted me to clean up after it.

I opened the door to the basement and was walloped by the odor. The putrid stink was a nasty mix of sulfur dioxide and methane. The rotting smell of death. It smelled like a box of bad choices.

Down the stairs, there they lay. A mangled mess of dead and rotting rodents. An empire of death that had produced the thick stench hanging heavy in the air. A million years of evolution and a short lifetime of shitty jobs flashed before my eyes. This is what my life had come to.

***

Rats can take three weeks to decay.

I had raised and slaughtered chickens and pigs, butchered beef and lamb, and maybe even stabbed or shot a man, but rats freaked me out.

Rodents always had this *I'm going to climb on you in your sleep and eat your lips off* feel. I am usually ok with dead things. It's a little weirder when they're warm. And when there are hundreds of them . . .

***

A female rat can mate 500 times with various partners during the six-hour period of receptivity. This happens 15 times a year. A pair of rats can produce 2000 offspring in one year.

Flies buzzed. So many, they created a hum. They laid their eggs in the dead flesh so it could nourish the newly hatched maggots. Some of the rats seemed to move; they were so filled with wiggling creatures. Many of the bodies deflated like a basketball that would see no more bounce. Others are blown up like a balloon, ready to pop. Maggots eat dead flesh and ignore the living. They begin in the stomach, then move to the head. The head eaten away, a small puddle in its place. The fur becomes matted and lifeless, then seems to float like pussy-willows as the flesh beneath begins to disappear.

I gagged. And gagged.

Back in the kitchen, I fashioned an apron into a face mask. Donned two sets of rubber gloves. Some plastic goggles and a long-sleeve sweat-shirt made up the rest of my bio-hazard suit. Alfred burst in with some woman. "Don't use all of my rubber gloves," he said, pawing the lady's backside. "He's my cook and exterminator," he told her. They laughed at me and went back to the bar.

I went back down into the basement. As I reached for the first body, a cold front stormed through my soul, freezing me as if paralyzed. I hovered above my body. When my courage returned, I took a deep mouth breath and picked up the first corpse. The body broke in half, sending maggots flying everywhere and a shiver up my spine that almost snapped it.

I wretched in a way that summoned the gods of places called Hell, and the bile it produced would have melted steel. I wiped the spittle off my lips and realized half a rat carcass remained in my hand. The first into the black trash bag. Only a hundred or so to go.

Back in the kitchen, I boiled water. Hot water kills maggots. The worst rats got the water, then into the bag they went. I filled bag after bag and then hauled them out to the garbage.

"Where's Wolfgang?" I asked after eight hours of dead-rat wrangling.

"I fired him," Alfred said, "I'm going to sell the hash myself." And he set his new man purse on the bar and groped his lady friend, who giggled.

"Ok." I ran my hands down my arms and tried to shake the creepy feeling that clung to me like the smell of dead rats.

Alfred grinned and looked down his big nose at me like we were friends. Or like I was his trusty dog. He showed me where he kept his gun, a snub-nosed .38, behind the bar. He wanted me to have his back in case Wolfgang came back.

***

Rat-baiting was popular in 19th Century London and pitted man or dog against hundreds of rats. The champion bull terriers could kill 100 rats in five and a half minutes.

On the way back to the barge, I stopped by the peep show to see the lady on the spinning bed. I called her Mary, but didn't know or care what her real name was. She was the patron saint of my life; isn't that fucked yet? Her invulnerable eyes stared into the void as many sorry-ass men fed coins into the slot to keep the curtain from lowering in their booth. Somehow it always cheered me up.

It took me two more days to clean out the basement. On the third day, Wolfgang came back. Alfred greeted him with his stupid overconfident grin. It offered no protection. Wolfgang reached into those hippy boots and pulled out a Walther PPK. He shot Alfred in the crotch. The rumors seemed accurate, although now the infamous python was in two pieces and not in working order.

Wolfgang stuck the pistol into his waistband and grabbed Alfred's man purse off the bar. He opened it up, grabbed a handful of bags, stuck them in my hand as he passed me, and headed for the door. "Take it easy kid. Love the hair."

Alfred was crying and moaning rudely like a baby that wouldn't shut up. I imagine being shot in the genitals hurts, but going on and on about it was tiresome. He urged me to get a doctor and an ambulance and call the police. I wasn't in the mood for all this drama and being bossed around like this. I opened the till, took the money owed me, and left, careful to step over the piece of his infamous member no longer attached.

I hoped a rat would eat it.

JOHN BOVIO (Twitter / X: @john_bovio) is a writer, artist, and chef. His work has appeared in various publications and galleries around the world. He lives in Oakland, California.

JUNE 2024 PROMPT — Home is where the noir is. This month, we're looking for stories set at home, wherever that is. Apartments. The suburbs. A townhouse. An RV. Under an overpass. We all need to lay our head somewhere, and while we imagine it to always be safe, sometimes that's just wishful thinking.

A Process

Maggie Nerz Iribarne

On her way through the familiar lobby, Margaret passed Super-intendent Kevin, or K-man, as Phil used to call him. He twisted in his swivel chair, his legs spread, knees loose, flowing with the rolling movement. He looked her right in the eye, said, *Good morning*, but did not produce her name. She forced one confident glance before moving with purpose to the stairwell. No worries about K-man, she thought. K-man didn't remember or notice anything special about her. K-man hadn't moved from his perch in all the twenty years she'd lived in the building, except to plod across the lobby to shovel doughnut holes down his throat at the occasional coffee social.

It had been a year since she'd entered this stairwell, but the flesh-colored paint still caused a slight anxiety creep. Margaret tilted her head, scanning the zigzag of railings to the rooftop seventh floor, remembering how as a young graduate student, a newlywed, this building had stood as a brick symbol of hope and promise, straight and steady like a bookmark holding a page in a favorite novel. It said, *I'll keep you safe, far away from your silly drunken mother and distant father and perverse brother.* In the beginning she believed herself safe within this building. She believed herself safe with Phil.

On the first floor, the lingering scent of some unknown person's body odor overcame the space. Phil's smell, Margaret thought. In the beginning, he was a firefighter, hunky in his black boots and flame-resistant jacket. He'd responded to another of her mother's small fires, holding court in their linoleum nightmare kitchen and smiling at the sweet sadness of the scene. On their fourth date, he shared how impressed he was with Margaret's *smarts*. He held her thin body in his powerful arms, whispered into her hair, *I'll take care of you, protect you, forever*. His smell wasn't repellent then. It was juicy, real, a comfort.

The crater Phil punched in the second-floor stairwell wall remained, a spiderweb of cracks emerging from a dented center.

That first time, the time Margaret said she'd like to make Thanksgiving herself to avoid their respective families, she'd been shocked by Phil's eruption of anger. As though there was no choice but to knock her senseless if she remained near his rising fist, he pushed on her shoulder with his left hand and punched the wall with his right. Later, after apologizing and enveloping her in a stifling hug, he asked her to read to him from his high school copy of *Romeo and Juliet*, which she did, although she was a nineteenth century gothic person, not a Shakespeare person, but it was all the same to Phil. At the end of their plodding, plundering sex, she gazed past him, feeling a numbing sadness at the sight of their wedding photo propped on the television stand.

On their old floor, the third, she slowed, her legs growing heavy as she remembered those final years living in the building, all the times she didn't want to return home. She'd dragged her feet each day, finding one more thing to research at the library, walking one more circle around the block, running one more errand. Phil grew a beard, finished his degree, and became a science teacher. His scent turned sour. At four o'clock each day, he held court at the dining room table, a constant, marmoreal presence, his blood red pen hovering above quizzes and tests. At dinner he'd regale her with stories of his prowess in the classroom, how the kids adored him, how someone of his caliber was so *necessary*. Watching *Jeopardy,* he'd sit tense and upright in his chair, yelling over Margaret's answers and saying *that's what I meant* when the correct answer was called. He'd developed opinions, commented on the wastefulness of Margaret's endless research compared to his useful profession. After dinner he rose behind her at the kitchen sink, a thick horny tree, bare and breathing, his limbs scratching, entrapping her.

On a whim, Margaret opened the sixth-floor door to check for the black cat, but a look to the right and left proved fruitless. Its owner, Mrs. Oponski, was dead.

Margaret had grown close to her elderly neighbor, visited her every day, enjoying her offers of sweet wine, homemade soups, stews, and salads. Mrs. Oponski possessed quite an indoor garden and had a way in the kitchen.

Mrs. Oponski makes things taste good! she said with her thick Polish accent. *Why don't you leave him?* she said.

I'll never finish my dissertation if I leave, Margaret said. *I can't support myself. Not yet.*

Why can't you finish?

I don't know. I want to. I just—

Mrs. Oponski held both Margaret's hands in hers and recited the Hail Mary in Polish.

Zdrowaś Maryjo . . .

It was Mrs. Oponski's idea, what happened to Phil.

Margaret burst through the seventh-floor door, out of the confining stairwell into the fresh May air. Phil had teased her about her fear of heights. He *was* a fireman, after all. *I'm used to putting myself in harm's way,* he often bragged.

Little did he know, Margaret thought, Mrs. Oponski's soup would prove more harmful than any tall, fiery building.

She pushed the rush of memories of that last day, of gasps and gags, flailing hands, a spilled bowl of borscht, a gaping mouth, dead Phil's dead weight.

Planes careened overhead, cars zigzagged on the ground below, voices lifted up on the wind, but Margaret ignored it all, moving decisively to the rooftop's silent center, the sagging symbol of her once-beleaguered heart.

She unlocked the defunct greenhouse door with the key Mrs. Oponski gave her, of which she had promised there was only one. The door whined as she pushed it open, exposing a grey, muffled light, a heavy musty smell. Inside, cracked clay pots, rusted rakes and spades were scattered about, abandoned, forgotten, remnants of the building's better days.

She approached the corner table, pulled back the tarp laid one year before.

There he was, blue-gray Phil, smelling no different than the rest of the place, of must, of dust.

He *had* said he wanted to donate his body to science. Yes, he is coming along nicely, Margaret thought, the skeletonization stage well underway.

She needed to share this day with him.

At the worst moments of their marriage, she believed he would never change, she could never change him, their circumstances. Look at us both, utterly transformed, she thought. She'd put on a few pounds, colored her hair red, had a new skeleton tattoo etched on her right shoulder.

"I'm finished with you now, Phil. I'm useful, and you're useless."

She removed her graduation cap from her purse, leaned it against Phil's diminishing skull, shading his hollowed eyes. She tucked the tarp around him. Then, she moved away, locked the door behind her, leaving Phil there, forever.

Margaret's graduation gown fluttered as she flew down the stairs, spiraling down the building's weathered spine, like vertebrae bulging, bursting beneath her hurried steps.

MAGGIE NERZ IRIBARNE is 55, lives in Syracuse, NY, writes about witches, priests / nuns, the very, very old, struggling teachers, neighborhood ghosts, and whatever else strikes her fancy. She keeps a portfolio of her published work at https://www.maggienerziribarne .com/.

JULY 2024 PROMPT – It's a time for gatherings and cookouts, so this month, we want your stories about food. That restaurant that's been open for 20 years despite never having any customers. A baker's deranged attempt to perfect their blood pudding. A delivery order gone horrifically wrong. Extra rare or well done, if it's about food, we want it.

A Li'l Something Extra

Ashley-Ruth M. Bernier

The ol' time saying declared that the way to a man's heart was through his stomach, and everyone knew Tyrell Cockburn loved to eat. Given his impressive girth and the feats of engineering he achieved whenever he stacked his plate at a buffet, the joke on-island was that the "way" to his stomach was four lanes wide with a couple of overpasses—although it was the kind of joke that lived in text messages and whispers, muffled and quiet so it would never get back to his grandmother. St. Thomas hadn't been ruled by a monarchy since Denmark sold it to the U.S. in 1917, but everyone understood Adina Cockburn was the closest thing on the rock to royalty. Ridiculous last name aside, the Cockburns had managed to maintain a number of high-value properties in Charlotte Amalie's Historic District, and their sprawling estate at the top of Skyline Drive remained a visible reminder that the family money was hadal-level deep. This was why, after Celine had gone on her fourth date with Tyrell, her mother decided it was time for a visit to Auntie Paloma.

"Actual auntie, or jus' Auntie-out-of-politeness?" Celine asked as her mother's ancient Toyota struggled its way up a serpentine hill on the island's northside.

"Li'l bit of both. Auntie Paloma used to be married to your great-uncle Albert," her mother explained. She didn't turn her face from the road, but Celine could see her mother roll her eyes. "Not that his ass deserved her. We can all agree on that, so there haven't been any hard feelings over the years."

Celine considered this. Great-uncle Albert died decades before she was born, and no one talked about him much—or, at least, talked about him positively. As for Auntie Paloma, her name always came up under very specific circumstances. Those circumstances usually involved a daughter who was a little inexperienced in the kitchen, a possible fiancé in the picture, and a mother itching for some grandchildren.

"Listen, Auntie Paloma's been helping young ladies catch and keep husbands for almos' half a century at this point, okay, dahlin'?" her mother said as they pulled up to a pretty little home at the top of the hill. It wasn't the Cockburn mansion by any stretch, but it felt like paradise to Celine—an expansive porch wrapped around a well-kept yellow house, mature mango, genip, and gooseberry trees in the front yard, and views of the Brasses and Hans Lollik Island in the distance. "Jus' go in her kitchen an' try to *learn* something from her. You could be a feast for Tyrell's eyes all day long, but eventually, the man's gon' need to consume some actual food."

Although she didn't say as much, Celine knew her mother was right. Every date with Tyrell had included detours to restaurants and food trucks. He'd flashed that dazzling smile, pearls set in the deep amber of his complexion, and shrugged his massive shoulders each time. "A man's got to eat," he'd said, and proceeded to annihilate a saltfish paté or a plate of oxtail and potato stuffing. Indeed, he did. Celine could make a decent baked mac-and-cheese, but to create the kind of spread for Tyrell to see his *forever* with her, she needed a miracle. And here she stood, that miracle, five feet tall and 100 pounds; with eight decades of culinary wisdom hiding behind patient brown eyes.

Celine was welcomed with a hug from Auntie Paloma, along with a cup of lemongrass tea and wedge of guava tart. After they'd waved goodbye to her mother and settled at the mahogany kitchen table, Auntie Paloma asked a question.

A little smile spread over the old lady's face. "What is it that you want, honey?"

Celine wasn't sure what to say. "Um . . . to learn how to cook? Tyrell loves a good bowl of kallaloo, so—"

"No, dahlin'." Auntie Paloma pulled her chair closer and took Celine's cinnamon-colored hands into her own. "I'm asking what you want . . . from him. *For* him. For you both."

"Oh." Celine hadn't stopped to think about this before. All she knew was what she felt whenever she was with him—a lightness, a breathlessness, a tingle she could only describe as pure joy. She let that feeling answer Auntie Paloma now. "I guess I want . . . his heart. I want his whole heart. A family. A life together. I want us to have all of it, Auntie Paloma."

The old woman nodded. "I see," she said gravely. "Then we have a lot of work to do." Her eyes flicked to a black and white photograph on the wall, and Celine recognized a much younger Auntie Paloma in the shot, hugging a tall and incredibly handsome man. They were standing outside of the Lutheran church in the heart of town, smiling at the camera like they'd just conquered the world. She squeezed Celine's hand and rose from the mahogany table. "First thing to learn is that deh trick to capturing a man's stomach—to capturing a man's heart—is to add a li'l something *extra*."

And so began Celine's months of tutelage under Auntie Paloma's experienced hand. Stews, sides, mains, desserts—when it came to Virgin Islands cuisine, Auntie Paloma knew how to do it all, and Celine was a quick learner. Soon, Celine could whip up a fried yellowtail with cornmeal funji, a plate of whelks and rice, hearty stew chicken or a fluffy batch of johnnycakes as easily as she could microwave popcorn.

Over the next few sessions, Auntie Paloma constantly reminded Celine to "Remember deh trick," and Celine had studiously watched the old lady's examples: an extra bay leaf added to oxtail gravy, some almond essence stirred into Vienna cake batter. A pinch of cinnamon in the guava tart crust, and the tiniest sliver of scotch bonnet peppers blended into the potato stuffing seasoning. "Anyone can cook well," she'd remind Celine. "You got to give him something he can't get anyplace else."

"A li'l something extra," Celine repeated one day, after tasting her pot of kallaloo and adding another dash of pepper to the rich green stew. She gestured to the picture on the wall. "Is that how you and Uncle Albert...what made him fall in love with you in the first place?"

Auntie Paloma had been ladling kallaloo into a ceramic bowl, but her body stiffened when Celine asked her question. A few seconds passed, long enough for Celine to wonder if she'd somehow broken the old woman, but when Auntie Paloma turned to face her, her smile was warm, her eyes clear and calm. "Yes, honey," she answered, handing Celine the bowl and a large spoon. "Your great-uncle, handsome as he was, had more than a few admirers aroun' deh island. But Albert did appreciate something different. A li'l something extra is exactly how I got him in the end." She slipped an arm around Celine's waist as Celine took her bowl of green stew. "And listen, my dear, I think you're ready to catch your own prince. Right through his stomach, honey. That's the way to his heart."

Later that month, Celine set a table for Tyrell on the modest porch of her parents' house and laid a feast fit for royalty out in front of him—fried snapper, a pot of kallaloo, potato stuffing, crunchy plantains, peas-and-rice, johnnycake; a pitcher of fresh-from-the-vine passionfruit juice, and three different tarts for dessert. And her love, of course, but Tyrell was focused on the meal. She'd found it, she realized as he filled his belly with thirds and fourths; that li'l something extra had found her the way to the first stop in her *forever*. His heart had to be the next destination. She wasn't wrong. Four months later, Celine officially became a Cockburn.

***

It was a very different Celine who sat across the table from her mother eighteen months later. She and Tyrell had moved into a well-built house with the same expansive harbor views as his grandmother's, but these days, it felt like a prison. Celine and her mother sat at an imported teakwood table in front of glass doors that opened up to the pool deck and endless southern views.

It was a beautiful structure that felt nothing like a *home*.

"You know," Celine's mother began as Celine wiped tears from her puffy eyes with a paper towel, "your great-uncle Albert was something of a scoundrel himself. Maybe a visit to Auntie Paloma would help?"

Celine protested at first. The old woman had been so hopeful for her, and Celine didn't want to return as a failure. Still, her mother had been persuasive, and before long, Celine was pulling her sleek new Mercedes into Auntie Paloma's driveway. No mangoes or plums in November, but the frangipanis and oleander plants next to the steps welcomed Celine with a fragrance that hung heavily in the moist northside air. Auntie Paloma's welcoming smile dropped the moment she took full notice of Celine, and within minutes, they were seated at the kitchen table, again with bush tea and guava tart.

As Celine told the whole sordid story, Auntie Paloma listened, weathered face impassive, brown eyes sorrowful. A few beats of silence after Celine's words ran dry, and then— "No children yet, I assume?"

"How could there be, when he barely even touches me?" Celine shook her head miserably. "I tol' you, Auntie, he has a different woman for every day of the damn week. He's high half the time, drunk the rest . . . and cruel no matter which. I can't bring a child into that."

"I see." The gravity in her voice was deeper, heavier than it had been when she'd used the same words in their first meeting. "Celine, what is it that you want?"

Tears flooded Celine's eyes. "I think I want his heart . . ."

Auntie Paloma sighed. "You want deh heart of a man who treats you like trash?"

"No," Celine whispered. "I wasn't finished. I meant . . . I think I want his heart to stop beating entirely."

The old woman sat silently for a moment, and Celine wondered if she'd gone too far. If she'd let her rage fuel words that weren't supposed to be let out into the world. If the old woman would shrink away, appalled and disgusted.

Auntie Paloma ultimately rose from her chair and walked over to the picture on the wall. "Albert had his moments, too," she said quietly. "He had several . . . paramours of his own, and when he'd drag himself home from the bars mos' nights, well, he also behaved like a pig and a brute. I felt the same way you did."

"I'm not sure you understand, Auntie. I meant—"

"I understand perfectly. You want his heart to stop. And deh way to a man's heart, dahlin', is through his stomach." Auntie Paloma walked across the room and opened a cabinet below the sink, one full of rows of dark bottles filled with liquids, powders, and leaves.

She picked one out and placed it gently in Celine's hand.

"Like *this* way. When you dice oleander leaves, it doesn't look like deh toxic plant we all know it is. Cut up like this, it could look jus' like any green seasoning. Mix it up in some soup, something hearty like kallaloo or spicy like goatwater, and nobody—not even the police or coroner—knows it's there. Your great-uncle enjoyed his rum and women, but he also loved my soups." She nodded down at Celine pointedly. "A li'l something extra is how I got him, in the end."

Celine considered the container in her hand. A quiet, breezy home with a cozy kitchen and mature plants outside had felt like paradise the first time she'd come here. With time and solitude, her new house could become this, too. Eventually. "Something he can't get anywhere else," she murmured.

Auntie Paloma smiled. "Exactly." She walked to the stove. "Let's cook, dear. You said he likes kallaloo?"

ASHLEY-RUTH M. BERNIER's (Threads / IG: <u>@armbernier</u>) stories have appeared in *Ellery Queen's Mystery Magazine, Black Cat Weekly,* **Stone's Throw***,* Smoking Pen Press, *Mystery Most Devious,* and *The Best American Mystery and Suspense 2023*. Originally from St. Thomas, U.S. Virgin Islands, Ashley-Ruth writes mysteries highlighting the vibrant culture of her home island. She currently lives in North Carolina with her husband and four children, where she teaches first grade and finds few things more valuable than uninterrupted writing time and the perfect cup of tea.

Ice Hit Trinity

Vincent Marshall

D rip.

Drip.

Her sweat dropped onto him. Droplets skimmed across the heat of his skin like ripples during the Solstice on a lake in Arkansas humidity.

Thrusts forced more drips, more ripples. Their breath pulsed together in unison. The headboard smacked the wall, rattling the floor of the trailer, as if the tectonic plates themselves were rubbing together, pleasure for the town to feel.

Alanna flung her blonde hair back. Looked into the sweet brown honey of Colt's eyes as he stared up at her. She felt herself match his smile– a mirror of lust matching equally missing teeth. It reminded her of black keys on a piano.

Colt smacked Alanna on her ass as if to tell the horse to pick up the pace. Alanna followed the order. She bucked and bucked as the sweet heat of the room rose to the temperature of the sun.

Colt smacked her ass again. She pressed one hand on his stomach and one on his leg behind her to steady herself. Her pace increased and for the first time she heard him let out a moan. It excited her more. The sound and the friction and the deep angle of his position sent shockwaves into her groin, up her spine to the top of her neck. As she screamed, he screamed back. The pace became rapid as they finished in an animalistic shriek of ecstasy together.

Alanna fell off her bronco and nuzzled next to him, out of breath. A crinkle of crisp paper crackled under their backs. Their chests rose and fell in rapid succession. Colt lifted his arm to move Alanna's hair off his chest. A couple of one-hundred-dollar bills stuck under his forearm and elbow causing Alanna to giggle.

"I never fucked anyone on ten thousand dollars before," Alanna said, plucking the bills off Colt. She flung them upward and the two watched as they descended like green leaves coming to the summer ground after a windstorm.

"Would hope not, babe," Colt said. He slapped his hand down on the mattress and fresh new bills stuck again. He shook his hand and bills fell onto Alanna sticking to her cheek.

"You sure we did right?" Alanna asked him.

Colt took a beat. He let the words hang in the fever of the bedroom. Alanna felt his chest rumble under her ear as if they'd went another round.

"My uncles," he finally said, "getting away from them is the best thing anyone can do."

Alanna found a chill hidden in the heat. She'd met one of the uncles inside the trailer months back. She sat on the loveseat behind a coffee table missing one leg, making it look like a redneck chiropractic table. A jar of potpourri used as the table centerpiece laid sideways on the ripped and brown-stained carpet where the leg finally gave way. Colt called him "Unc." She couldn't recall his name, or, looking back on the interaction, any of the others' names either. Her impressions of him were that this was a man to be feared and needed. He held all the keys, literally and figuratively. His age and creepiness amplified her concerns when Colt accepted another delivery job. She felt his eyes all over her. She wore a skinny thin purple skirt and crossed her legs in front of her. He pulled on his scruffy chin and licked his chapped lips. She dared not dream of getting inside his head. She knew she wouldn't like what she saw of herself. When he left, she'd felt the urge to shower.

Colt told her how, in the beginning, he made small runs to Little Rock and Jonesboro, and a year later took on deliveries across the southern part of the country. Six months later he made a small drop at a house party down in Heber Springs and it's there where they met.

She wasn't like other tweakers. Her beauty remained intact despite the meth mouth beginning to show its ugly side. She recognized his look immediately. The lust they shared turned into more than either of them could ask for. She was smitten and so was he. She moved in with him a couple months later.

Dawn to dusk in those early days were filled with nonstop fornication. But then Colt dipped his toe in his own supply. It'd been a suggestion she made to him when she was in a deep three-day bender and her body refused to rest. He told her he wanted to feel what she felt. A rip off the new coffee table he had bought at an antique store, and a new love made its way into their lives. An unholy alliance. Alanna, Colt, and Crystal were inseparable.

Colt broke off pieces for himself and Alanna here and there. He made sure those misdeeds stuck to out of state drops. Ones where no one would see him again unless they meant to. Despite the addiction and his loins clouding his judgment, he kept to that code until one tweaked out idea led them to where they were now.

"Well, what you thinkin?" Alanna asked him. She made swirls with her fingertip around his chest hair and over his malnourished ribcage.

Colt exhaled. "I'm thinkin' I'm gonna take a piss and then I'm coming back in here and we doin' that again."

Alanna pulled away from him with a laugh. She watched her no-ass-having Colt get off the bed, then let out another cackle as she noticed the Hundreds pasted to his backside, including one hanging near his taint. She howled, tickling under his balls making a "ling-a-ling-a-ling" sound as she grabbed the bill.

Colt swiped away her hand in embarrassment. "The hell you doin', woman?"

"It's like it turned into a thong along your ass." Alanna rolled onto her back laughing, until tears fell from her eyes and down into her hair, mixing into the sweat of the sex.

She eyed Colt as he flung the rest of the bills off his body and retreated to the bathroom. He kept the door open and she observed the stream hit the toilet between his legs. All she could do was shake her head. She loved that son of a bitch. She dreamed of their life on the road. Plastic bags of cash sitting in the back of the truck cab as they headed out west towards a new life. A life away from his uncles. From Crystal. From the humidity that enveloped the trailer because the window AC unit stopped. From the johns who knew her real name. From all the pain the Ozarks put her through.

Colt had taken her out behind the trailer the day he told her the idea of a better future. He lined up vodka bottles on the barbed wire fence post of the adjacent farmland. He handed Alanna a .22 rifle and showed her how to aim, or so he thought. In rapid succession she knocked down all four bottles. Four shots, four hits.

She told him how when she was young, her father used to take her down to the creek and set up whiskey and vodka bottles to show his little girl how to shoot. First with a .22 rifle he inherited from her grandfather. Next came pistols and revolvers. Alanna knew her way around the handle of all types of weaponry. Colt later told her he had never been more turned on than when she fired off more rounds, taking out more bottles. His plan A had a plan B and the perfect partner to execute it with.

Alanna marveled at the fantasy as the man of her dreams, her White Knight, finished up in the bathroom. She cocked her head and spread her legs. The fever of the room seemed to target between her thighs. She was ready.

A crash struck the bathroom window. All Alanna saw was the splash. The splash of blood that exploded as if a balloon filled with crimson paint popped where Colt had a head. The bathroom went from rusted gold and copper to red as a stop sign. His body jerked to the right as he slammed down on the toilet. His feet were all she could see. Her fantasy of running away turned into a nightmare.

Before Alanna could sit up, the gates of Hell seemed to open and engulf her, a Hell of broken glass, splintered wood, and a symphony of bullets.

Alanna rolled off the bed and army-crawled her way to the living room. Her breasts and knees and elbows gathered rug burns as she moved through the trailer. Abruptly, the shooting stopped turning the bedroom into Swiss cheese.

Against the door stood two AR-15s and a 12-gauge shotgun. Alanna grabbed one of the ARs first and chambered a round. She didn't have time to get dressed. Not right now. She pulled up and pointed out the large window frame of the living room and scouted the outside. Three pickup trucks were parked in front of the trailer next to Colt's.

No movement.

She guessed the shooters were at the back of the trailer.

The silence meant reloading.

She crept back into the bedroom and pulled on a pair of jeans and a T-shirt. Seeing Colt, she choked back tears. He'd want her to fight. Cry later, babe, his voice rang in her ears. We talked about this, too.

Dressed now, she chambered the other AR and cocked the shotgun. She cocked her head and gritted her teeth. Her eyes tightened as she waited to hear the outsiders. A beat or so went by until she realized she needed Colt's keys. Hearing nothing happening outside, she crept back into the bedroom again and did a quick scan.

She spotted the keys under the bed, the gold ring glistening in the sun that shone through one of the bullet holes. She crawled her way to the bed and the trailer erupted in hellfire again.

Alanna scrambled her way into the living room and waited. She knew when the shooting stopped, she could make her run. She pulled one AR sling around her back. She kept the shotgun at home. She needed the succession hits the ARs brought. No time for one-and-done shots from the shotgun.

Alanna put the key ring in her teeth. Her bite cracked a tooth. The adrenaline obliterated the pain.

The silence fell upon her, urging her to make her move. She opened the door and peeked. Seeing no one, she ran. She heaved the driver-side door to Colt's truck open and threw herself in, lying down behind the dash where she waited for a response. The nothingness went on for eternity. She pulled herself up and peered over the dash. No one. She grabbed the keys from her teeth and put them in the ignition. She stopped. Her life for the past year and a half flashed before her eyes. Colt's smile. Colt's rail-thin naked body. The road head on a delivery, the late nights in the back of the truck at Lake Chippewa. The masked robbery of his uncles. The last time she saw the lust in his eyes looking up at her. The future they planned together.

Fuck Colt's uncle.

Alanna bit down on her tongue and swung the truck door open. She grabbed both guns and stomped her way towards the back of the trailer. She put her back to the trailer and slid her way along the side as a shield. She crept up the opening of the back field when a gun barrel came around the edge of the trailer. Without missing a beat, Alanna batted aside the barrel, stepped around the corner, then pulled the trigger. Quick shots. Three, center mass. The body fell. Behind the falling body, she saw a sea of men in jeans and buttoned-down shirts, like an armed rodeo let out. She recognized one of the men as Colt's "Unc." The others were likely cooks or dealers or both. The more the merrier. She didn't care.

Alanna unloaded. Bodies flew back and off to the sides. Some went for cover that wasn't there. She felt the gun give out empty and she pulled the other AR around her to begin again. By the time the second AR emptied, the rodeo was over, the ground behind the trailer as red as the dirt under a family of deer gutted in December.

Alanna fled back to the truck and got in. She thought about going back in for shoes and the money and setting everything on fire as she stuck to the plan to head west, but she couldn't stomach seeing Colt that way again. She wanted to keep the good memories intact. She turned the ignition key and heard a click. The truck didn't fire up. She turned the key one more time. Nothing.

Alanna panicked. She pulled the door handle to get out and check under the hood when the driver-side door slammed shut against her shoulder. She forgot Colt had two uncles. The dealer. And the one who ran a body shop.

The man said something to her through the glass, but she didn't hear him. Instead, the last thing she heard was the window crash and she felt the heat against her temple as the sweating sun went dark.

VINCENT MARSHALL (Threads / IG: @vincentmmarshall) is an award-winning journalist living in Arkansas with his wife Shauna and their five children. When he is not writing he's either reading, fishing or out on the hiking trail and never passes up the opportunity to wear a hoodie.

Behind the Deli

Leslie Elman

Behind the deli, four guys sat on plastic crates and played poker with cards slick with grease from the griddle. Sunset triggered the sensor on the floodlights bolted to the strip mall wall.

Tom brought his Dodge Charger to a stop and killed the engine. The guys behind the deli took no notice as he entered the dry cleaner through the rear door. Once inside, he waited, screened by a curtain of plastic-wrapped suits and dresses.

At the counter, Milton scanned the barcode on a customer's receipt. The motorized clothing rack engaged, starting a swaying parade of garments—up from the basement, around the back and down to Milton, who plucked the customer's order off the line and hung it on a hook within her reach.

The customer glanced at the Vandals' schedule affixed to the back of the store's cash register. "Ugh, they're starting again?"

"Pre-season in two weeks," Milton told her.

"Followed by six months of listening to my husband complain about them."

"You never know. It could be a good season."

The woman groaned. "They stink. They always stink. Wish I was paid what they're paid to stink like that."

Spying Tom amidst the dry cleaning, Milton squeezed a sympathetic smile in his direction.

When the woman was safely out the front door, Tom stepped out from behind the clothing. Milton said, "Coach, good to see you," and handed Tom a bunch of garments on hangers twist-tied together. The dress on top didn't look familiar, but Tom knew it was futile trying to keep track of Aubrey's wardrobe. Aubrey did a lot of shopping.

"Gonna be a good season?" Milton asked cheerfully.

Tom shrugged. "We might surprise some people."

He left the cleaners the way he'd come in. Milton had offered him that courtesy a few seasons back, after a particularly unpleasant encounter with a fan. The fans took their football seriously here, claimed the team like they owned it—tossed you treats when they were pleased with you and kicked you when they weren't.

Outside in the parking lot, the snap in the air smelled like football—cold, hard, invigorating. Tom closed his eyes, inhaled through his nose, and exhaled through his mouth: the yoga breaths Aubrey taught him. *In, two three four. Out, two three four.* "Let the dark stuff go. Let the lightness in," she said. *In, two three four. Out, two three four.* He pictured autumn leaves scissoring lazily to the ground and felt lighter—or maybe just light-headed.

When he opened his eyes, he saw the emerald green ("Green like money, Tom-Tom") Mercedes AMG with its "F-N-D" license plate parked in a darkened corner of the lot. Tom unlocked the door of his Charger, tossed the clothes onto the back seat, and was halfway into the driver's seat when he heard a man's voice call, "Tom-Tom!" The floating autumn leaves in Tom's imagination hit the ground and were crushed to dust. He stepped out of the Charger.

"Why're you throwing those pretty clothes around like trash, Tom-Tom?" Effendi Wilson was all muscle and mouth. A one-time golden prospect who hadn't lived up to expectations, he was the best the Vandals had, and he would never be good enough.

"Wilson," Tom said flatly.

Wilson sucked air through his teeth in rebuke. "Hang those pretty dresses up right, man," he said. "You don't want me tellin' Aubrey you treat her stuff like that."

Tom narrowed his eyes, but even at a respectable six-foot-one, 190, he knew he wasn't about to win a stare-down with a man-mountain like Effendi Wilson. He flipped the driver's seat forward, fished Aubrey's dresses out of the back seat, and hung them from the assist grip.

"Tom-Tom." Wilson played a drumroll with his fingertips on Tom's head. "You gotta watch a woman like Aubrey. Old dude like you. You don't treat her right, she's gonna go looking around." Wilson shifted his shoulders, rearranging his muscles. "Plenty for her to look at. Know what I'm sayin'?"

Tom set his lips together, ran his tongue over his teeth, sucked air through his nostrils, said nothing. He got back into the Charger and started the engine.

"You listen to what I'm tellin' you, Tom-Tom." Wilson grinned a filthy grin. "And tell my girl Aubrey I said hi."

Tom reversed the car abruptly, causing Wilson to flinch. "Ooh! Big man, Tom-Tom!" Wilson pushed aside his suede jacket and placed his hands on his hips. Tom glimpsed a handgun tucked into the waistband of Effendi Wilson's jeans. Shifting into drive, he pulled away, tires crunching over gravel and crushed glass on the cracked asphalt. In the rearview he saw Effendi Wilson walking toward the strip mall. The guys behind the deli were picking up their crates and cards and calling it a day.

***

On the practice field, Effendi Wilson broke through the line, turned to receive a pass, bobbled it off his fingertips, and was summarily knocked on his ass by a defensive back before the ball hit the ground. He shook his head and chuckled. They ran the same play again. Again, Wilson went down on his ass, a little harder than the first time. You had to be pretty damned obnoxious for your own defense to want to lay you out during practice.

Effendi Wilson was that obnoxious.

He trotted to the sideline where Tom stood with only his clipboard to defend him. "Tom-Tom!" Wilson grinned and played a drumroll on Tom's head with the same fingertips that couldn't hold onto the ball. "You get those pretty dresses home to Aubrey?" Wilson hovered behind Tom, close enough so that anyone who couldn't hear them might think they were discussing the practice. "Bet she looks good in them dresses." Wilson sucked lascivious air through his teeth.

Tom kept his eyes on the practice field, where La'Shawn Stillman, a new recruit wide receiver, deked around his coverage and made a fingertip catch. "You watching, Wilson?" Tom said. "That's how it's done." The rookie, face glowing with a sheen of sweat, headed to the sideline, where his teammates greeted him by pounding on his shoulder pads.

"*You* don't tell *me* how it's done." Wilson spat something frothy on the ground at Tom's feet before putting on his helmet and heading back onto the field.

A cold wind lifted the hood of Tom's jacket off his back. He closed his eyes, inhaled through his nose, and exhaled through his mouth until the lightness reached him.

Effendi Wilson caught the next pass he was thrown, pumped his fist, and shouted "F-N-D!" like the license plate on his green-like-money Mercedes. Then he pointed the football at Tom as if it were a loaded weapon.

***

The first time Tom saw Aubrey was in a hotel bar, which was neither as tawdry nor as titillating as it sounds. She was on the road doing safety compliance checks at a factory that made ceiling fans. He was on the road to meet a junior college kid the scouts thought might make it in the pros. (The factory passed; the kid didn't.)

The hotel bar was the only place in town that served food past 8 p.m. Tom had a burger. Aubrey ordered the house salad and wound up eating most of Tom's fries. He was honest and lonely. She was smart and bored. They enjoyed being together and there was genuine affection between them even if their marriage—the second for both—hadn't managed to eliminate his loneliness and her boredom.

His job as wide receiver coach of a professional football team was something other guys would covet more than any neighbor's wife. And yet— In his mind, he heard Aubrey say, "I thought it would all be more fun."

It might have been more fun if the Vandals were a winning franchise or in a top-tier city. They were neither. The working-class city was unlikely to change for the better. As for the record, much of it came down to bad luck or poorly calculated gambles, like signing Effendi Wilson to a four-year contract.

***

Tom wasn't surprised when the offensive coordinator called him in to talk about a personnel problem, but he was steamed when the OC said the problem was Tom himself.

"I'm hearing complaints," the OC told him.

It was pointless to ask "Who from?" but Tom did anyway.

The OC waved off the question. "Get the wideouts doing their jobs."

"Or you'll find someone else to do mine?" Tom knew the team could replace him a dozen times over for what it would cost to replace Effendi Wilson. "Going on record here, I was always against picking up Wilson."

"Good for you," the OC said. "Play the hand you're dealt, Tom."

When Tom told Aubrey about his conversation with the OC, she reacted as he knew she would, expressing empathy yet open to the possibility that the problem might be something Tom did, or didn't do, or could have done. "Three sides to every story, right? Yours, his, and the truth. Fendi's got an ego, sure, but he's all right. He's always nice to me."

Tom noticed that Aubrey was wearing the dress he'd fetched for her from the cleaners; the one he hadn't recognized. He noticed that she called Wilson "Fendi" like a fan—or a friend.

"What's that look?" she asked.

"Nothing," Tom said. "It'll work out. Don't worry."

"Do I look worried?"

No, Tom thought. She didn't. She never did. It was one of the things he loved about her.

***

Effendi Wilson's Mercedes pulled into the parking lot behind the strip mall just as Tom was tossing the dry cleaning into the back seat of the Charger. Meeting Wilson out here in the suburbs once could be a coincidence; two consecutive weeks seemed intentional.

The driver's side door of the Mercedes opened, and Wilson stepped out. "Tom-Tom! How you doin' Tom-Tom?"

"What are you doing here, Wilson?"

"You think I'm following you? Yeah, that's right. I wanna be where you are, Tom-Tom." Wilson snickered. "Don't you worry about what I'm doin' on my own time. You got other things to worry about. Your job. Your wife . . ."

Wilson reached out to pat Tom's head.

Tom clocked him on the jaw.

For a moment, time froze.

"Damn, Tom-Tom!" Wilson's face registered disbelief. He rubbed his jaw, shook his head, bent at the waist with his hands on his knees. "*Damn . . .*"

Blood pounded in Tom's ears and throbbed through his fingers. "You don't mess with my job. Or my wife, *Effendi*."

Wilson was still doubled over when Tom pulled out of the parking lot.

*****

Effendi Wilson missed the next morning's practice. Tom noticed, of course, but Wilson was a no-show often enough that no one remarked on it until they broke for lunch and one of the trainers asked, "You heard what happened to Wilson?" Tom put a forkful of pasta in his mouth and shook his head.

The trainer said, "Someone in the suburbs beat the crap out of him." Tom chewed until the pasta liquefied in his mouth. He wasn't sure he could swallow. "Turns out Wilson was playing high-stakes poker in the basement of some deli. Out where you live." Tom choked the pasta down and coughed. "Maybe he owed somebody money. Or shot his mouth off one too many times. They found him the parking lot beat to— You all right?"

Tom nodded. *In, two three four. Out, two three four.*

"So, looks like you got a job, buddy," the trainer said. Tom squinted, not comprehending. "Replacing Wilson," the trainer said. "How's that kid Stillman working out?"

In, two three four. Tom considered the prospect of a season without Effendi Wilson. *Out, two three four.* He pictured La'Shawn Stillman's face glowing with sweat and promise. He felt the lightness reach him. "Stillman," Tom said. "Yeah. Good. He's good. He'll do the job. No problem."

LESLIE ELMAN (Bluesky: @leslieelman.bsky.social) is an Edgar Award-nominated writer whose short fiction has appeared in *Ellery Queen Mystery Magazine*, *Alfred Hitchcock's Mystery Magazine*, *Vautrin*, and *Mystery Magazine*.

OCTOBER 2024 PROMPT — Every town has a legend of a haunted place, and in most cases, those legends and haunted places involve a crime. This month, we want stories about legends, real or imagined, the crimes that inspired them, and the way those legends affect those living in their shadows. Make it dark. Make it gothic. Make it undeniably **Stone's Throw**.

On the Air

Justin Walsh

Of course the kids say Norah haunts the lookout at Galley Tops. Of course they do. It's the sort of story she and I would have spread and maybe believed a little bit when we were 12. At that age, a local ghost legend is dark and irresistible, like a cave.

So when Samantha tells me what the kids have been saying, I'm not offended on Norah's behalf. In fact, I like the idea a little. If she's there, I tell Samantha, she'll make a beautiful ghost.

Samantha visits me once a week, when John and Angela—my live-in carers—have the afternoon off together. The time she spends with me earns her credit towards a health science unit at school, and that's OK. She's 15—the age Norah was when she died.

I had just turned 16 then, and I'm twice that now. I've never left Conleigh—I couldn't if I wanted to—but the thing is, in all these years, I've never felt Norah near. Not at our old schools, not at the playgrounds or the sports field or the shopping center or at church, not on the street where her family lived, and definitely not by her grave.

I've never been back to the lookout. I don't think anyone would have taken me if I'd asked; anyway, it was closed for ages because of rock falls. A few years ago, a big boulder dropped into the little car park and that's when the park service started doing stabilisation work further up the hill. Samantha shows me an article in the *Chronicle*—lately they've rebuilt the platform and the barrier, extended the parking area and put in ramps instead of steps. Now I can go there if I want to, and I decide I will.

I want to fill this Norah-sized hole inside me. I've always wanted that. I'm not hoping to be visited by her ghost, but I want to feel her nearby. Within me or around me, maybe coming in on the air, just now and then. That's the kind of spirit Norah would have wanted to be. So I think if she's waiting for me anywhere, it might be up at Galley Tops.

***

Was there a moment when we could have saved ourselves? Did we make a dumb decision, did we miss a chance to step out of the asteroid's path? These are the things I think about. We were sitting on a bench in the riverside park, late on a cool September evening, when Reynolds and Kepper parked their big brown van nearby. We didn't recognize the van; they weren't locals.

I guess we could have just walked away before they got out of the van, or run when they came over. But we stayed. Maybe it was because we had just been talking about boys, and Reynolds—anyone would agree—was good-looking and charismatic, like the lead singer in a band. Soon we were in the back of the van, both of us winded by gut punches and slapped into a daze, wrists fastened with thick white tape. Reynolds had a big knife and a wild laugh. Kepper drove, nervous.

They took us out of Conleigh to the south, away from the river and into the hills. They parked in a lane I'd never seen before. Later, Detective Todd told me it was a driveway going to a derelict farmhouse. It was dark by then, and the only light came from the van's cabin when the doors were open.

***

On the weekend, John says the weather will be fine over the coming days and asks if I'd like to go out. Let's go for a drive outside town, I say—if we go on Wednesday afternoon, maybe Samantha can come. John books the minivan and checks the air in my outdoor chair's tires.

Wednesday comes, it's cool and there's a breeze. We decide the trip is on and Samantha texts to say she'll come if we pick her up at school. Angela rugs me up, rigs my bottles—fluids in and out—and asks again if I'm sure the lookout is a good idea. It will be fine, I tell her. There's nothing to be afraid of; there are no bad things left to happen.

Up at Galley Tops, John wheels me down the minivan's ramp and I feel the air moving all around us. While Samantha stows the ramp and locks the hatch—one of those *demonstrated competencies in clinical support*, she calls them—John walks my chair in a slow circle. I can't turn my head far, so he always gives me what we call 'the three-sixty tour' when we arrive somewhere.

The scene is familiar and different. I saw this place a few times as a kid, always in daylight. I couldn't see much here on the night Norah died. Today, it looks like a cleaned up, polished version of the old lookout. What hasn't changed is the air—the way it seems to flow up out of the valley, folding around us, audible in the trees overhead.

'Ready to go to the platform?' John asks.

'Sure,' I say. 'Sam, lead the way.' And we go down the curving ramp, across the little bridge and out towards the cliff edge.

I ask John to park me in the middle of the platform. I don't want to look over the edge. But he and Samantha walk over to the barrier.

'Hey, Norah,' I say out loud. 'Are you here, girl?' Samantha turns and looks at me. John keeps looking out into the valley. The air moves around us, then there's stillness. For a moment.

***

Kepper held the knife for a while, but he didn't hurt us. A psychologist told me later that Kepper thought he was in love with Reynolds, and he found sexual intimacy with him by enabling the rapes.

When Reynolds was finished with me, he dragged me around to the back of the van, where Kepper was sitting beside Norah. I looked at Norah, wanting her to meet my eyes so I could let her know *I'm OK, and we're going to get out of this.* But her head was down.

Reynolds shoved me towards Kepper.

'She's got short hair, pretend she's a boy,' he said. His laugh was mad. 'I'm gonna need some time with this other one.'

He grabbed Norah by her ponytail and started to pull her away. I charged at him then, but my shoulder just bounced off him. He let go of Norah, gripped my taped wrists in one hand, held me arm's length and smashed his other fist into my jaw. I heard a sound like rocks splitting and I don't remember anything clearly after that.

Later I think I was conscious for a few minutes in the back of the van. I sensed we were going uphill, Norah was beside me, breathing but not moving at all, and the men were in the front. Then we had stopped and Norah was being pulled out through the back door. I tried to say her name but everything was wrong in my mouth, my teeth and gums all jammed up, blood over my lips. Kepper looked in at me and said something like, *hey, it will be over soon.*

Then Reynolds was back. He pulled me out and hoisted me over his shoulder. I remember it was really dark and we were going down some steps, wind in the trees, that sound filling the air and I thought *the lookout oh Jesus he threw Norah over I'm next, our father who art in heaven I pray the lord my soul to keep.*

As Reynolds tipped me over the railing, I snagged my fingers in his long hair stand that's what saved me. My grip broke but I slid down the cliff face rather than going out into the air. Then I was falling free for a moment, until I slammed onto the spiky rock that broke my fall and my spine.

I have only scraps of memory after that. There was pain, like one big pain around and inside me, but nothing that connected to any parts of my body. The sky got lighter and I knew I was cold but I couldn't feel the chill on my skin. Later, when the sky was bright blue, someone high above me was shouting. Then there were some ropes hanging and a man wearing an orange helmet was in the air beside me, talking into a radio.

***

On the drive back to town, Samantha asks me what I think about ghosts.

'You first,' I say, which is what Norah always did when someone asked a question like that. *People who ask for your opinions mainly just want to tell you theirs*, she'd said.

'I don't know,' she says. 'There's the body and the soul, right, and life leaves the body when you die, but maybe not every soul is ready to leave here at the same time. Maybe it needs to stay?'

'Well, I'm not religious,' says John, who is old enough that he's lost a lot of people. 'So I don't see it as being about souls. When someone dies, they're mostly gone. Some people say you live on in the memories of the ones you leave behind. But I don't know if that's really living.' He pauses for a moment. 'What I think is, we only really die when everyone who knew us has died too. As long as someone's thinking about you, you're partly still here.'

'What about you, Lesley?' Samantha asks.

'Let me think about it for a while,' I say. 'I'll get back to you when I know.'

The truth is, I'm feeling something change inside me. I'm feeling *Norah,* for the first time since she died. It's not that I sensed a ghostly presence up at the lookout or anything like that. No invisible hand touched my cheek; no disembodied voice murmured in my ear. But as we get close to town, something inside me seems to settle into place. A gap is closing over.

That night, after Angela has put me to bed, I check—and I can't feel that Norah-sized hole anymore. She's not with me, but she's not utterly absent like before. *You're just away for now*, I think. *I'll feel you again soon.*

***

I didn't have to testify at a trial. Detective Todd told me that Kepper had agreed to cooperate when they promised he could serve his sentence in the same prison as Reynolds. Reynolds was going to plead not guilty, but the prosecutor had the idea of bringing me to a meeting with his lawyer. I think the lawyer looked at me in my chair, strapped upright with my head braced to a column, wires and tubes going everywhere, and realized his client should not let a jury decide his fate. So they took a deal, too.

Reynolds, who was 23, got life without parole. Kepper, already in his forties, got 28 years. As soon as the sentences were formalized in a hearing, they were sent to prisons at opposite ends of the state.

Reynolds didn't live long. Another prisoner beat his head to pieces with the seat of an exercise bike. Detective Todd told me that he'd driven out to give the news personally to Kepper, along with a little cardboard box. His squad partners had pasted together a shard of an off-white china bowl that they thought looked like a skull fragment, some dark hair snipped from a wig and a scoop of pork mince. The warden let him give the box to Kepper—*thought you'd like something to remember Reynolds by.* He left Kepper howling and cursing.

I got a smile out of that story. Believe it or not, I can be lighthearted about dark things. I've been medicated against depression for the last ten years. These days, I don't really have strong feelings about anything.

But I'm glad to have Norah with me again. I'm sure I can find her whenever we visit the lookout. And I hope that one day, if I'm sitting by an open window at home, she might meet me here, too.

Then she'll leave again, the way she left the first time, on the air.

JUSTIN WALSH lives on the land of the Guringai people in eastern Australia. A long-time avid reader of crime and spy fiction, he's trying his hand at creative writing.

NOVEMBER 2024 PROMPT — It's election season, so this month we want to see stories about the government, its power, and how it can put its thumb on the scale. Whether it's a cop with a chip on their shoulder, a zoning board member that cannot be reasoned with, or a congressman saying one thing then doing the other, we want to see your stories about the little guy, and what happens when they come face to face with unaccountable power.

Fragments of a House

Mike McHone

"We've been going back and forth all day. You've gotta stop this. Hear me? I got two dead deputies, Jason. Two. You can't put the whole town in this mess."

"There wouldn't be a mess if the town would've done what was right."

"Jason, you and I—"

"I'm not coming out, Will."

"Then we're coming in."

"Good luck."

Excerpt of the official phone record of the Monroe County Sheriff's Department.

***

On the morning of August 7, 2023, a homeless man by the name of Danny James decided to shoplift blue jeans at the Kohl's on Telegraph Road in Frenchtown Township, Michigan. After store security noticed he'd picked up three pairs of Levi's 501 jeans, Danny, 29, ran from the store and headed toward Elkton Drive in the Arbor Creek subdivision about a mile and a half away. When he saw a sheriff's cruiser at the end of the block, Danny panicked. He noticed the door to the attached garage of a nearby house was open. He darted inside. He tried the door that led into the house and discovered it was unlocked.

The house was owned by a widow named Samantha Scott. Samantha was working in the flower garden of her backyard and didn't notice Danny until she went inside to grab a glass of water. She tried to run, but James grabbed her by her arm. Samantha screamed. She fought against her invader, but he was too strong and far too desperate.

Ben Wilson, a retiree who lived next door, heard the scream and saw Samantha trying to pull away from a strange man in her kitchen. Wilson called 911.

Within thirty minutes, a dozen sheriff's cruisers had arrived on Elkton Drive. A negotiator came soon after, and tried to bargain with James, asking him repeatedly to surrender. He refused. However, at noon, the unexpected happened. James yelled out of an open window that he would let Samantha Scott go, since, in his words, she didn't "look too hot." Samantha made it outside, collapsed on the front lawn, and was rushed to the hospital.

Upon Samantha's release, Danny refused to speak to the authorities any further.

Seeing no alternative, Sheriff Will Borman ordered his deputies to enter the house. Windows were broken and smoke grenades were tossed inside. Police kicked in the back door, made their way through the home, and found Danny James in the spare bedroom at the back of the house. In his hand was what the sheriff's deputies initially believed to be a gun.

They fired.

When deputies inspected the body, they discovered the object in James' hand was simply an antique bottle of cologne in the shape of a flintlock pistol. Samantha's son, Jason Scott, said in an interview with detectives, the bottle had belonged to his deceased father. Both his parents were avid antique collectors. Sheriff Borman would not speculate as to why James picked up the bottle. It is reasonable to assume, however, that perhaps James, with a criminal record that extended over a decade and the possibility he'd be put away for the rest of his life because of the standoff, saw no way out and had a death wish.

It was, however, not to be the only death that day. Samantha Scott died later in the ProMedica Regional Hospital emergency room of a massive coronary. She was 70.

The bill for Samantha Scott's funeral was just under $6,000. The damage to the home due to the broken windows and drywalling and repainting to cover up the bullet holes was estimated to be $4,000. The cost of the blue jeans stolen from Kohl's amounted to a little over $200.

When Jason Scott filed the insurance paperwork after his mother's funeral, he found out the policy would only cover part of the bill. When he asked for a reason, it was explained that once the insured reaches 70 years of age, the payout is reduced by half. Samantha's policy was for $10,000. Her birthday was six days prior to her death.

No one from the township council or the sheriff's department attended Samantha's funeral.

When Jason filed paperwork at the same insurance company to get money for the repairs on his mother's home, they refused to pay, saying the damage was caused by "government intervention" and they were not legally bound to cover the costs. It was, they said, the responsibility of the sheriff's department to pay for the damage.

He took his concerns to numerous township representatives. Every reply was similar. The township was not obligated to pay for the damages considering the sheriff's department was within their right to utilize whatever force they deemed necessary to neutralize the threat Danny James posed to Scott's mother and the community at large. The first conversations Jason had were polite, if tense, but eventually, every encounter would devolve into yelling and screaming, leading deputies to escort Jason from the building.

Over the ensuing weeks, Jason sought legal counsel, but no lawyer would hear his case, stating the legalese in the insurance paperwork and the township bylaws was clear.

Having lost his job at the recently shuttered Gorman Steel factory, and with his savings dwindling fast, recently divorced Jason Scott, 38, had no idea what to do or where to turn.

An excerpt from Chapter One of Small Town Fury: The Two Standoffs at Arbor Creek *by true crime podcaster and bestselling author Edward Keck*

***

"He moved in a couple two, three months after his ma passed. I heard he couldn't afford his apartment anymore after his ex cut out on him, so he moved in here. He was quiet. Kept to himself. I guess he just spent a lot of time trying to patch up them bullet holes inside, and repainting. I never had no trouble with him in the seven, eight months he lived there.

"Until that one morning . . .

"I was in my living room cleaning, had the windows open, and I hear these people arguing. I look and I see Jason going at it with two deputies. Deputies tell 'em the windows need to be fixed, else he'd get a fine. Jason had some wood slats duct taped over 'em. They said the windows needed glass, not wood. Jason says he can't afford it. Tells them the township should pay for it. They say the township shouldn't have to. It went on like that for a while, screaming, hollering, they threaten to arrest him. Finally, Jason just says, 'Okay,' goes inside, and he . . . He came back out with a pistol and started shooting. Just . . . snapped right out there in the daylight, started shooting. He shot that younger fella in the head like it was . . . like it was nothing. He hit the other one in the back, but I heard from somebody later that he made it to his car and was able to, uh, call for help before he . . . ya know.

"I ain't proud to say it, but it scared the hell out of me. As soon as I saw him shoot those guys . . . I ran upstairs, and I, uh, stayed in my bedroom for a bit. I didn't know what to do. I mean, I knew I should've called 911 but I just couldn't. That day when that, uh, whatchacallit, that shoplifter came, I didn't think twice about calling, but . . . seeing that one boy's head just . . . I felt like if I called anybody, hell, if I did anything, Jason would find me and . . .

"I know it sounds stupid, real stupid, but that's what I thought.

"Anyway, it started to get dark, and the rest of the department showed up again.

Taken from an interview with neighbor Ben Wilson

***

"yall did him dirty. outta be ashamed."

"2 dead cops. Lol. Good start"

"the government shoulve cleaned up their mess."

"F**k him. He does something like that, he gets what he deserves."

Comments from the Monroe County Sheriff's Facebook page regarding the incident.

***

"I don't want to do this, Jason. Let's end this peacefully."

"I ain't coming out. I already said."

"Listen—"

"I'm hanging up, Will. You wanna talk more? Walk your ass in here."

-click-

Excerpt of the official phone record of the Monroe County Sheriff's Department.

***

After disconnecting the call with Sheriff Borman, further attempts to reach Scott went unanswered.

At seven pm, Borman ordered tactical teams to move into the house with the express order that Scott was to be taken alive. As it was with the deadly standoff with Danny James, a series of smoke grenades were tossed into the home through the wooden slats covering the windows.

Scott did not exit the home.

Two teams moved in. Team A entered through the front, Team B through the back. The main floor of the home was swept.

Scott was nowhere to be found.

Team A checked the attic while Team B moved toward the basement. Sergeant Ramona Ariza took point. As the team made their way into the stairwell, Ariza saw something at the bottom of the stairs.

The body of Jason Scott.

He was in a fetal position, his Colt .38 resting inches from his body. From her vantage point, Ariza saw no blood, and no one claimed to have heard a gunshot. She assumed at first Scott was, as she stated, "playing possum," but as she descended the stairs, she noticed Scott's neck had an odd shape. She looked closer and saw a bone had broken through the back of his neck.

It was then Ariza discovered a board on a center step on the stairs was loose. She surmised that once the Sheriff's Department tossed in the smoke grenades, Scott tried to make his way to the basement. He stumbled on the loose step, pitched forward, hit his head against the concrete wall, and snapped his neck.

An excerpt from Chapter Twenty of Small Town Fury: The Two Stand-offs at Arbor Creek.

***

"We can sit here all day and go through the whole fucking thing, but it won't change what happened. Should those deputies've gone out and threatened him with a ticket? Not in my opinion. But they weren't stepping over their bounds either.

"And it's not like they were ordered to go out there. They drove by, saw the house in the shape it was in, decided to stop and talk to the owner. I mean, they were young, new to the department. They probably didn't know what happened with that shoplifter. They were just doing their job.

"You've got to look at it both ways. If we would've helped him pay for the repairs, it would've opened the door to all kinds of ya-hoos coming in, wanting to get their places fixed up. That's what our lawyers said, for the most part.

"But on the other hand, it was—what?—three, four grand to fix it up? We spend more than that on advertising for the fucking county fair, and we couldn't figure out a way to shuffle a few dollars around?

"When you get down to it, just because we were obligated to turn him down, doesn't mean we should've.

"I mean, Christ, if I'd have known three grand would help avoid all this, then, shit, I'd have gone into my own pocket and paid for the repairs myself.

"All this over some broken windows . . ."

From an interview with an anonymous Monroe County employee.

***

I'm sorry for everything. I don't blame you for leaving. You always said I need to control my anger. You were right. As always.

I love you forever. You were my world.

A note addressed to Jason Scott's ex-wife Linda, found on the kitchen counter in his mother's house.

***

"I heard the Sheriff knew him somehow. I don't know how. He comes in here a lot. I asked him about it once. He said he didn't wanna talk about it."

Lori, a server at The Grafton Bar and Grill.

***

"Borman needs to step down."
  "wasn't the sheff's fault his ma died."
  "thoughts and prayers."

Comments from the Monroe County Sheriff's Facebook page.

***

"No comment."

Sheriff Borman after a request for an interview.

***

Jason,

Glad to be graduated. Finally! Ha! Loved playing b-ball with ya all these years, my man. You're the best three-point shooter ever. Can't wait to see what happens next.

Call me. Lets hang sometime.
-Will

An inscription found inside Jason Scott's high school yearbook.

MIKE McHONE's (Twitter / X: @mike_mchone; Instagram: @mike_mchone) fiction has appeared in *Ellery Queen*, *Alfred Hitchcock's Mystery Magazine*, *Dark Yonder*, *Mystery Tribune*, *Mystery Magazine*, **Rock and a Hard Place**, the Anthony Award-nominated anthology **Under the Thumb: Stories of Police Oppression**, Edited by SA Cosby, and elsewhere. A former journalist, his articles, op-eds, and humor pieces have appeared in the *Detroit News*, the *AV Club*, *Playboy*, and numerous other outlets. He is the 2020 recipient of the Mystery Writers of America's Hugh Holton Award and placed twice on *Ellery Queen's* Annual Readers List. His short story "The Last Ruined Night," originally published by **Rock and a Hard Place** was cited as a Distinguished Story in 2024's *Best American Mystery and Suspense* anthology. He lives in Detroit.

DECEMBER 2024 PROMPT — It's time for Jingle Bell **Rock**. For December, we want stories about music. Whether it's musicians in a very tough spot, a record collector who will do anything to get that rare LP, the secrets that lurk in relationships between bandmates, or the traditions and legends of specific musical subcultures, if it's about music, we want to roll with it.

What Ever Happened to the Cracker Jacks?

Tom Andes

For Brett Evans

It turns out being an icon is not all it's cracked up to be. Just ask any child star whose life winds up a sad parade of drugs, straight-to-DVD movies, and behind-the-scenes documentaries, or any boyband veteran who ends up the subject of an episode of VH1's *Behind the Music*.

Never mind one who throws himself off a hotel balcony in New Orleans.

It started for us on a talent show on public access TV, Channel 27, back in Boston. Nirvana was riding the charts—Kurt was still among us—and New Jack Swing was hitting hard. The winds of change were upon us, and the producers wanted to cash in on this latest trend before it went the way of houseguests and fish left too long in the fridge. They wanted kids who could dance the shoeshine and the shuffle—in other words, little players and New Jacks—but they wanted them to be white.

By now, I guess you've read about the aftermath. For years, my brother was a regular feature on *TMZ*, and Perez Hilton should've cut us a check for all the traffic we directed his way. In these days of Elon and X, we've faded from public consciousness, except for the occasional ironic revival, or when somebody posts an article on a slow news day: "What Ever Happened to the Cracker Jacks?"

But now, with a gun in my hand in a hotel room in New Orleans, with a suitcase full of cash on the bed, with sirens sounding out the window and the flashes of a hundred smartphones popping below me on the sidewalk, I know we're going—as the kids say—viral.

***

"He's got it coming." That's what I told my brother, Kevin when I walked into room 206 in the St. Peter Hotel thirty minutes ago, before I pistol-whipped our former manager, Mourad Malati, then gave my brother the gun to finish him.

Why was it so easy to convince Kevin? Maybe it was the coke. Maybe Kevin had been dreaming of this since he was a teen. Maybe it was just that Mourad was a First Class, Grade A piece of shit.

And so, even though I was a little surprised when Kevin pulled the trigger, plugging Mourad in the gut—my brother's aim must've been off since he was still cuffed to the bed—I was looking forward to watching Mourad die a long, slow death.

Kevin had been doing so well, too. After that last stint on *Celebrity Rehab with Dr. Drew*, my brother had managed to stay out of jail, and out of the tabloids. But when a guy falls, he falls hard, especially from the heights we'd climbed.

"The fuck," I said. For a hot minute, back in the day, my brother had been laying pipe to Britney Spears. Now, one of his hands was cuffed to a king-sized bed in the same hotel where Johnny Thunders had died; my brother's shit-streaked tighty-whities pulled down his thighs, tears staining his tattooed cheeks. He grinned at me, showing off his new, diamond-crusted grill.

"I shot him." He was sniveling, coked to the gills.

"No shit." I grabbed his phone from the floor next to the bed. I took the gun back, too.

***

Depending on who you asked and who he was talking to, Mourad was either Syrian or Russian. He'd been the visionary, the one who'd seen us dancing on that show, *Boston's Got Talent*—five Southie teens doing steps we'd picked up in classes at the Roxbury Community Center. Credit where credit's due: if he'd seen an opportunity, he'd seen the future, too. Like Sam Phillips and Colonel Tom Parker before him, like Eminem a few years later, he knew what white America would tolerate pumped into its living rooms.

Not that we were Elvis Presley. Not that between the five of us, we had half as much talent as Eminem's got in his pinky finger.

Kevin had been the star, and Mourad's favorite. In this age when these revelations drop on the daily, you know where this is going, don't you? Back then, we'd all been diddled by clergy, teachers, uncles. Kevin was being groomed for success by Mourad. Well, he was being groomed in other ways, too.

If we did suspect, so what? Kevin was our hot ticket out of a life of petty crime. The best thing in front of us was working the docks, a foregone conclusion that we wouldn't achieve half of what our fathers had. And all our dads had done was slap the shit out of us and our moms on their way to drinking themselves into early graves.

Yeah, all the signs were there, the drug use, the depression. But the worst part was the fact my brother wanted to take himself seriously as an artist. You'll remember his solo record, which was held up for ridicule in those early days of the Internet, receiving a rare zero-star review in *Pitchfork*, the critic saying my brother was like Vanilla Ice without the redeeming features, calling the record a modern-day minstrel show.

Truth was, we hated him. Young as we were, success went to our heads. On that last world tour, Kevin insisted on his own bus, like he was the star, and we were the backing band. Like he was Mick and Keith, and we were the rest of the Stones. Like he was James Brown, and we were the Famous Flames. Like he was Michael—

Well, you get the picture.

After the solo record, he said he was going to rehab. Half the shows on his breakout tour had been cancelled due to low ticket sales. It was a flop, a faceplant of epic proportions, his career written off as DOA.

"Guess you needed us after all," I told him, months later, when he suggested a reunion show. I'd dabbled in music production, done a stint as a backup dancer on Janet Jackson's *All For You* tour, but my future held a life of straight jobs. Mourad had negotiated our contracts. When the band broke up, I had enough in savings for a down payment on a house in Southie, two blocks from the Old Colony Housing Project where we'd grown up.

Not like Kevin, the star, with the fat solo contract.

"Please." On the other end of the phone, he was sobbing. After all those years of seeing him in the limelight, I was happy about it, like when I'd read those pans of *Jacked 4 Lyfe*. "I just need a little cash to get me into a facility."

"Why don't you call Mourad, since you've always been his butt boy."

And I hung up on him.

***

Maybe I couldn't have known how those words would hurt him. But even if I didn't *know*, I *knew*. No surprise when years later, he sold the whole sordid story to *Us Weekly*. It was supposed to be the beginning of his comeback, his public rehabilitation, but he was too far gone with the nose candy.

All that gangsta stuff? It was a front. The face tattoos, the gold teeth, the wifebeater tank-tops, *thug life* on his fists, he wore that mask to convince the world he wasn't the sensitive kid who'd dazzled a studio audience on *Boston's Got Talent*, peaking on public access TV at age 17.

***

All of which brings us back to this hotel room in New Orleans, where half an hour ago, I showed up to find my brother hand-cuffed to the bed, like I'd walked into a scene from a weird European movie—something out of Lars von Trier, that one with Björk and the trains.

"Just couldn't stay away," I told my brother, "could you?"

Kevin was shaking his head. "I needed money, man."

"Where'd you get the dough for that grill, those new teeth?" Disgusted, I kicked the tray with the lines of blow they'd been doing across the room, Kevin's eyes bugging.

"Dude." He might've hoovered the stuff up from the carpet. "Lighten up."

For years, when his bank accounts were empty, credit cards maxed out, when he relapsed and needed cash to stay on a bender, my brother went back to Mourad, his Daddy Malati.

In the corner, Mourad was coughing. Blood flecked his lips, black fluid seeping from a wound below his heart—gut shot, like a fat, horny buck.

"I made you," he said, "made you what you are."

As if that was something to be proud of, making the Cracker Jacks.

"Should we call an ambulance?" Kevin's teeth were chattering: a symptom of shock, as I knew from my EMS training, since I had to get a real job.

I sat with the gun. "We're going to watch him bleed out."

"Every time I called and asked him for money," Kevin said, "he'd make me do this."

"Somebody help." A foam of blood was on Mourad's lips. The room smelled of his intestines, whatever organs the bullet had pierced. He tried getting to his feet, grunting as he fell against the wall.

"Bro, get me out of these handcuffs." In Kevin's face was the beginning of a realization. "Hey, what are you doing in New Orleans, anyway?"

***

And yeah, part of me did go to look out for him. I knew he couldn't stay clean, knew Mourad would make Kevin an offer he couldn't refuse. Poor fucker, maybe he thought I'd come to patch things up, make amends.

As if.

No, I've been following Kevin since I got to town, and I came here for that suitcase, the money Mourad gives Kevin every time they get up to their little shenanigans

That was the plan: boost the cash, ice Mourad, and leave Kevin on the hook for the murder beef.

But now, damn my conscience, I want to get Kevin out of here, too.

***

I take the cuffs off. It isn't my fault, what comes next.

If you've seen the *Behind the Music* episode or read the articles in *Buzzfeed*, you're familiar with the official version, which culminates in a tragic murder-suicide: after years of abuse, the washed up one-time protégé and frontman of a chart-topping boyband turns on the promoter who took him off the mean streets of Boston, killing him in cold blood before throwing himself out a New Orleans hotel window during Mardi Gras.

The story's got sex, sleaze, intrigue.

Like most stories, it's half true.

***

Maybe it's the drugs. Maybe after decades, he can't take it anymore. Maybe he knows he'll get done for murdering Mourad, or he doesn't have the stones to live with himself after killing the guy. Not even if I was the one whispering in his ear, telling him to do it.

He's out the window like a streak. In the glare of those cellphone flashes, in his dirty underwear, he balances on the wrought iron railing. I go after him, leaping toward that balcony, but those flashes are popping, and I don't want to be in the frame.

"Kevin," I shout.

He looks over his shoulder, and I swear, he has the same expression he did that day on *Boston's Got Talent*, when he knew he'd nailed it, securing our future, changing our lives.

If only we'd known how they would be changed.

I see it again, as if in slow motion. Can I say—do—anything to stop him?

But like when we were kids, Kevin's the star, the one out front, hogging the limelight.

"Not worth it." Those are his last words.

"Don't—"

I'm still saying it when he jumps.

Out the window, below the railing, under that blank piece of sky where my brother was, people scream.

Holy fuck.

I grab the suitcase. Time to go, but not before I finish Mourad, a bullet to the temple, more merciful than he deserves.

I wipe the gun, toss it on the bed, and run, slamming the door behind me.

This is Kevin's last viral moment, and I want no part of it.

TOM ANDES (Twitter / X: @thomaseandes; Instagram: @thomasandes) wrote the detective novel *Wait There Till You Hear from Me*, forthcoming from Crescent City Books in 2025. His stories have appeared in dozens of publications including *Best American Mystery Stories 2012*, *Ellery Queen's Mystery Magazine*, and *Santa Monica Review*. He lives in Albuquerque, where he is a working musician, performing solo and with several bands. He is also a freelance editor, writing coach, teaches, picks up catering shifts, and pet sits. His two acclaimed EPs of original songs will be rereleased on vinyl by Southern Crescent Recording Co. in 2025. He can be found at tomandes.com.

EDITORIAL BIOGRAPHIES

R.D. SULLIVAN (Stone's Throw Editor; Bluesky: @thebigleblues ki.bsky.social) is a writer of fiction, comedy, and letters to the editor. A recent East Coast transplant, she is enjoying the trees that aren't on fire. Her writing has been featured at *Fireside Fiction Magazine*, *Shotgun Honey*, and *Tough*, as well as in the *Killing Malmon* and *Murder-A-Go-Go's* anthologies. She has also published an erotic story about a ham sandwich. True story. You can track her down over at govneh.com.

PAUL J. GARTH (Stone's Throw Annual Editor; Threads / IG: @PauljGarth) is an editor for **Rock and a Hard Place Press**. His short fiction has been published in *Thuglit, Tough, Needle: A Magazine of Noir, Plots with Guns, Crime Factory*, ***Rock and a Hard Place Magazine***, and several other anthologies and web magazines. His novella, *The Low White Plain*, part of the "A Grifter's Song" series, was release in June 2022. He lives and writes in Nebraska, where he lives with his family.

ROGER NOKES (Editor-in-Chief; Threads / IG: @StantonMcCaffery) writes fiction under the pseudonym Stanton McCaffrey. His short stories have been featured in *Dark Yonder, Mystery Tribune, Vautrin, Shotgun Honey*, and more. He has stories forthcoming in *Reckon Review* and *Tough*. He has published two novels: *Into the Ocean*; and ***Neighborhood of Dead Ends***. His short story, "Will I See

The Birds When I Am Gone," is featured in *Best American Mystery and Suspense 2024*.

ALBERT TUCHER (Contributing Editor; Facebook: @albert.tucher) is the creator of sex worker Diana Andrews, who has appeared in more than 100 hardboiled stories in venues including *The Best American Mystery Stories 2010*. Her first longer case, the novella *The Same Mistake Twice*, was published in 2013. In 2017 Albert Tucher launched a second series set on the Big Island of Hawaii, in which *Pele's Prerogative* is the latest entry. He is a past president of the Mystery Writers of America NY Chapter, lives in New Jersey, and loves NJ Turnpike jokes.

JAY BUTKOWSKI (Managing Editor; Threads / IG: @jt-butkowski) is a writer of fiction, an eater of tacos and an amateur pizzaiolo who lives in New Jersey. His stories have appeared in on-line and print publications, including *Shotgun Honey*, *Dark Yonder*, *Tough*, *Yellow Mama*, *All Due Respect* and *Vautrin*. He is a founding editor at **Rock and a Hard Place Press**, an independent publisher chronicling "bad decisions and desperate people." He's also a father of teenage twins, a doting husband, and a middling pancake chef.

ROB D. SMITH (Editor; Threads / IG: @RobertDominicSmith) is a common man attempting to write uncommon fiction out of Louisville, KY. He is an Honor Roll recipient for Outstanding Stories in the *2024 The Best Mystery Stories of the Year*. Currently an editor at **Rock and a Hard Place Press**, his work has appeared in *Apex Magazine*, *Shotgun Honey*, *Pyre Magazine*, *Thriller Magazine*, *Tough*, *Reckon Review*, *Vautrin*, and several other crime, horror, and specu-lative magazines, anthologies, and online publications. *Good-Looking Ugly* is his debut crime novel. Find his work at https://robdsmith.carrd.co/.

ASHLEY-RUTH M. BERNIER's (Acquisition Editor; Threads / IG: @armbernier) stories have appeared in *Ellery Queen's Mystery Magazine*, *Black Cat Weekly*, **Stone's Throw**, Smoking Pen Press, *Mystery Most Devious*, and *The Best American Mystery and Suspense 2023*. Originally from St. Thomas, U.S. Virgin Islands, Ashley-Ruth writes mysteries highlighting the vibrant culture of her home island. She currently lives in North Carolina with her husband and four children, where she teaches first grade and finds few things more valuable than uninterrupted writing time and the perfect cup of tea.

VICTOR DE ANDA (Acquisition Editor; Bluesky: @victordeanda.bsky.social) is a writer in Philadelphia who enjoys watching movies and searching for good Mexican food. His fiction has been published in *Dark Waters Vol. 1*, *Guilty Crime Story Magazine*, *Mystery Tribune*, *Shotgun Honey*, and *Punk Noir*, with more forthcoming. You can find out more at https://linktr.ee/victordeanda.

SUSAN JESSEN (Acquisition Editor; Threads / IG: @SuzJay11) enjoys reading, reviewing, and writing fiction of various genres. She received an MFA in Writing Popular Fiction from Seton Hill University. A former Priority Editor at *Flash Fiction Magazine*, she continues to provide editorial feedback during their quarterly contests. Her flash fiction has been published under a pseudonym in anthologies and magazines such as *The Arcanist*, *Lost Balloon*, and *Shotgun Honey*.

www.ingramcontent.com/pod-product-compliance
Lightning Source LLC
Chambersburg PA
CBHW020048310726
48970CB00007B/2465